KRIS
KRINGLE'S
Magic

KRIS KRINGLE'S Magic

DIANE STRINGAM TOLLEY

SWEETWATER BOOKS
AN IMPRINT OF CEDAR FORT, INC.
SPRINGVILLE, UTAH

This is a work of fiction. The characters, names, incidents, places, and dialogue are products of the author's imagination and are not to be construed as real.

ISBN 13: 978-1-4621-1105-3

Published by Sweetwater Books, an imprint of Cedar Fort, Inc., 2373 W. 700 S., Springville, UT 84663
Distributed by Cedar Fort, Inc., www.cedarfort.com

LIBRARY OF CONGRESS CATALOGING-IN-PUBLICATION DATA
Tolley, Diane Stringam (Diane Louise Stringam), 1955- author.
  Kris Kringle's magic / Diane Stringam Tolley.
      pages cm
  Summary: With the help of the elves, Kris Kringle and his wife, Rebecca, deliver toys to all the children in the world on Christmas Eve.
  Includes bibliographical references and index.
  ISBN 978-1-4621-1105-3 (alk. paper)
  1. Christmas stories, American. [1. Santa Claus--Fiction. 2. Elves--Fiction. 3. Toys--Fiction. 4. Christmas--Fiction.] I. Title.

  PZ7.T5747Kri 2012
  [Fic]--dc23

                                    2012026274

Cover design by Erica Dixon
Cover design © 2012 by Lyle Mortimer
Edited and typeset by Melissa J. Caldwell

Printed in the United States of America

10 9 8 7 6 5 4 3 2 1

Printed on acid-free paper

For my grandchildren,
Who never fail to show me
The magic of perfect love

PROLOGUE

*R*ebecca opened the door.

A neatly dressed young Elfa stood there, clutching a new leather folder to her green-coated chest.

"Ah, Dorothy! Just in time." Rebecca smiled and swung the door wide. "Come in!"

"I tried to give you a few minutes," Dorothy said rather breathlessly, stomping the snow from her warmly booted feet and stepping inside on a bright, hand-hooked rug. "I figured it would take you a while to say good-bye after Santa's liftoff."

Rebecca laughed. "You know me well, dear," she said. "I do like to speak to everyone after we wave Santa off." She pushed the heavily carved door shut.

"Come in, dear, and let's get comfortable, shall we? We've got plenty of time."

Dorothy laughed. "Yes, it'll be a few hours before Santa gets back."

Rebecca nodded. "It's usually a long night for

me," she said, sighing. "I'm sure it goes a lot faster for him."

"Mama always says that keeping busy is the best way to make time pass," the little Elfa said.

"Your mama is a wise woman," Rebecca said. "Now let's go in here, shall we? There's a spot for you to put your writing materials, and we'll be close to the warm fire."

"It *is* a chilly night," Dorothy said, grinning. "But what else can you say about the North Pole on December the twenty-fourth?" She glanced around the comfortable room. "Oh, Mrs. Santa, you have such a nice home!"

"Please, dear, call me Rebecca," Rebecca said. She followed the little Elfa's glance.

Gleaming pine logs formed the walls of the long room. A large, stone fireplace took up most of one side, its mantle covered with carvings and pictures and cherished knickknacks. Thick, hand-knotted rugs covered most of the wide, darkly polished floorboards. A massive oak desk, piled high with papers and books, stood at the far end of the room. The large, empty chair beside it was mute evidence of its owner's absence.

Other furniture in the room—chairs, sofas, and assorted small tables—was equally heavy, obviously lovingly carved and highly polished.

Dorothy sank into one of the two large chairs near the fireplace and dragged off her green knitted cap. She dropped it to the floor beside her and unbuttoned her coat. Then she pulled a sheaf of papers and two pencils from her satchel and placed them neatly on her lap.

Finally, she folded her hands together and looked at Rebecca. "So, where do you want to start, Mrs. San . . . Rebecca?" she asked.

Rebecca sat down in the chair opposite and smiled at the eager little Elfa. "Well, dear, you asked for this interview," she said, her eyes twinkling from behind her glasses. "Maybe you have some idea of what you want?"

"Oh, I do!" Dorothy said eagerly. "I want to know it all! How you met! Fell in love! Moved to the North Pole! Everything!"

Rebecca laughed. "That's a *tall order*, if you'll pardon the pun."

Dorothy's face puckered into a frown. "I don't get it," she said.

"Don't worry, dear, you will!" Rebecca said.

She leaned back in her chair and turned to look at the flames crackling quietly in the fireplace. "So. Where to start . . ."

Finally, she turned back to the little Elfa waiting patiently across from her. "I guess the best place to start is the beginning," she said.

Dorothy picked up a pencil and looked expectantly at her hostess.

"When Kris and I first met," Rebecca said. She smiled happily and brushed a hand across her eyes. "It was . . . oh, a very long time ago . . ."

CHAPTER ONE

"Hey! Who does Abel have with him?" Redheaded Bert pointed behind us.

Everyone turned for a look.

A tall, blond boy had followed twelve-year-old Abel Bauer from his house.

"I don't know," Margaret said, smoothing her fluffy gold hair and blinking her china-blue eyes. "But he is certainly handsome!"

Trust Margaret to notice that. She was only nine, like me, but was always following the boys around and smiling and making "flutter" eyes at them.

And they noticed her too. Because she was tall. Nearly a head taller than me. And pretty.

Self-consciously, I stroked a hand down my own long, rather nondescript, light brown hair and sighed.

"I think it's his cousin," Little Paul spoke up. "He and his mama are here to stay for the summer."

"Oh," Bert said. "Well, I guess that's all right."

I snorted. "As if it's up to you, Bert!" I said loudly.

Bert glared at me but didn't reply.

Bert and I had had dealings before, and he was rather hesitant to start anything with me again. His ego couldn't take two beatings by someone half his size.

Abel and his cousin joined us. "Hey, everyone, this is Kris," Abel said. "My cousin."

There was a chorus of "Hi, Kris!" and "Hello!" and "Glad to meet you!"

Then silence.

Everyone had obviously used up their conversational quota.

"So, Kris. Where are you from?" Bert finally asked.

Kris looked at him. "Germany, actually," he said. His voice was soft but oddly piercing. And he had a distinctly German accent.

"Oooh. Germany is my favorite place!" Margaret said, moving close.

He smiled down at her. "Good," he said.

"What does your papa do?" Bert wasn't going to be sidetracked. He was the self-proclaimed leader of our little group and he wanted to prove it to the new kid.

"I don't have a papa," Kris said.

"What? Why?"

I pushed Bert with one hand. "Stop it, Bert. Maybe it's something Kris doesn't want to talk about!"

Kris smiled. "It's all right," he said, raising his eyebrows and turning arresting blue eyes on me. "Miss . . . ?"

"I'm Rebecca," I said.

"Rebecca," he echoed, his smile widening. He looked at Bert. "My papa drowned," he said. "When I was just a boy."

"Oh." Bert was embarrassed, but he tried hard to cover it. "Sorry."

"It's all right," Kris said, kindly. "You didn't know."

"So what is everyone doing today?" Abel asked.

"We're going to raid Mrs. Schmidt's cherry trees," Bert said proudly.

"I don't have to tell you whose idea that was," I said, grinning.

The other kids laughed.

"Raid?" Kris said, frowning.

"Actually, Mrs. Schmidt leaves her trees for us to 'harvest,'" I said. "She's old and can't do it herself any more and doesn't trust anyone else to do it, so she lets us take what we want. All we have to do is leave a bucket of the best beside her front door every time we go into the orchard."

Kris's face cleared, and he happily joined us as we

started toward the last house on the block.

Every yard on our beautiful street of large homes was surrounded by a picket fence, neatly painted in whatever color the homeowner currently favored.

Mrs. Schmidt's was the same.

Everyone headed toward the front gate.

There, Kris stopped. "What's this?" he said. He was looking at a board, jutting out over the sidewalk, that was nailed to one of the gateposts . He glanced at me. "A sign?" He frowned. "There's nothing on it."

"Oh, it's just a measurer," I said, stepping past it as I headed for the gate.

"A measurer?"

I stopped.

Kris had one hand on the sign, which came up to him about chest height. "A measurer for what?"

I stared at him. "Well, for measuring!" I said.

He cleared his throat. "Measuring what?" he asked again, more slowly.

"Well, for Elves," I said.

He turned to look at me. "Why would we need to measure Elves?" he asked.

I blinked. Was he crazy?

"So we can tell who is welcome and who isn't," I said in my most practical voice.

"Welcome?"

Okay, he *was* crazy.

"Kris," I said, trying to sound patient, "we need those measurers to keep the Elves out."

"Out of what?"

"Out of everywhere they're not allowed to go." I was beginning to lose patience. "Honestly, Kris, don't they have measurers where you come from?"

"No."

I felt my mouth drop open. "But . . . how can that be? How do you know who's allowed and who isn't?"

"Everyone's allowed."

"Oh, that's just crazy!" I said. "You mean that the Elves can go wherever you go?"

"Exactly."

I shook my head. "Well, I'm just glad I live here," I said.

Kris shot out his hand and grabbed my arm.

"Ouch! Kris, that hurts!"

"You honestly agree with this?"

I managed to pull my arm from his strong grip. "Agree with what?" I said, rubbing the reddened skin. "That really hurt!"

Kris scratched his forehead. "I'm sorry. I didn't mean to hurt you," he said. He took a deep breath. "But do you really agree with this . . . this . . . *measuring*?"

"I don't understand why you are asking," I said. "Of

course I agree with it. That's how it's done!" I stared at him, "Well, except where you live."

Just then, Mrs. Schmidt opened her front door. "Hello, dears!" she called out, cheerfully. Then she turned away from us and scowled. "Here! Right here!" She stomped a foot. "Oh, you Dienes (she pronounced it "deeens," drawing out the word) are the stupidest creatures ever! Get out of the house before you make it unfit for me to live in!"

Two Elves came out of the doorway, heads respectfully bowed.

Mrs. Schmidt heaved a sigh of relief. "Now, can we start again?" she said.

The two Elves stood in front of her and waited.

"I asked you to fix the roof. The roof! Not the ceiling! Are you too stupid to know the difference?"

"We're very sorry, mistress," one of the Elves said, his voice high and squeaky. "But we noticed that the damage to the roof went through and into the house itself and we were just checking to see if it had damaged any of the interior rooms."

Throughout this little speech, Mrs. Schmidt moved her mouth and mimicked speaking, obviously mocking the little Elf.

"Well, then you should have knocked properly and asked me," she said, finally. "Do you think I want the likes of you inside my house? You'd steal me blind!"

I lost interest. "Let's go in," I said to Kris.

But Kris didn't move. He was staring at the trio in front of Mrs. Schmidt's comfortable home, his expression cold and fixed.

"Kris? It's nothing to do with us," I said. "Come on."

Finally he looked at me.

I nodded encouragement. "You know? Go? Join the others?" I made two little walking legs with my fingers and mimed walking toward the backyard.

But Kris still didn't move.

"Go on! Get out of here!" Mrs. Schmidt said to the Elves, waving one hand dismissively.

The two Elves disappeared around the house.

Mrs. Schmidt heaved a great sigh. She looked up. Seeing Kris and I still standing there, she smiled once more. "You two want some cookies?" she said. "I've been baking!"

"Oh, no thank you, Mrs. Schmidt," I said. "We're heading out back to raid your orchard."

"Oh, good," she said. "Have fun!" She went into the house, closing the door firmly behind her.

"Well, that's over," I said. "Come on, Kris. Let's go."

But Kris stayed where he was.

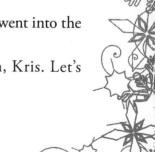

"Kris?"

He glanced at me, then put both of his hands on the measurer.

Suddenly suspicious, I moved closer. "Kris?"

He looked away for a moment. Then there was a sharp crack as, with a quick jerk of his hands, he suddenly ripped the measurer right off its post.

I jumped back and stared at the white board clutched in his strong hands.

Mrs. Schmidt came running out of her house. "What have you done?" she shrieked.

Kris looked at her, then deliberately lifted one knee, and smashed her measurer over it, neatly breaking the sign in half.

It was done so slowly that, at first, Mrs. Schmidt didn't know what to do. "Oh! Oh!" she said. She jumped up and down a few times.

Then she began to scream.

Within seconds, the street behind us was boiling with people.

A policeman forced his way through the crowd, finally coming to a breathless halt beside the still-screaming Mrs. Schmidt.

He put a hand on her arm, and she glanced at him, abruptly silenced.

She lifted one hand and pointed a knobby finger

at Kris, who simply stood there, the two pieces of her measuring board held casually in one hand.

"This . . . this . . . this . . ." She couldn't get any further.

"Take a deep breath, Mrs. Schmidt," the officer said.

She did so. "This . . . this . . . *hooligan* . . . destroyed my property!" she managed at last. "My personal property! I want him arrested at once!"

The officer turned to look at Kris. "Have you anything to say, young man?" he asked.

"No," Kris said, handing the two pieces of board to him.

The officer looked down at them. "What's this?"

"I think you call it a measurer," Kris said lightly. He looked at me. "At least that is what this young lady says."

"Kris!" I said in my loudest whisper as I shrank back behind the nearest person.

The officer glanced briefly in my direction, then back at Kris. "You . . . how did you get this?"

"I broke it off," Kris said.

"Broke it off?"

"Yes. It offended me." He glanced around at the crowd, letting his gaze rest on several Elves who were hovering in a small group apart from everyone else.

Then he looked back at the officer. "It should offend all of you."

I moved farther away, putting several people between me and the crazy boy from Germany.

"You see?" Mrs. Schmidt said. "You see! Loony as a sack of nuts!"

"I think that's supposed to be 'nutty as a sack of nuts,'" Kris said calmly.

"What . . ." Mrs. Schmidt sputtered into silence.

"Young man, if what Mrs. Schmidt says is true, you are in a powerful amount of trouble," the officer said.

"If!" Mrs. Schmidt said. "I watched him do it!"

"You saw him tear the measurer off your post?"

"Well . . . no. But that girl did! She was standing right beside him when I came out of the house!"

"Girl?" the officer surveyed the crowd.

"That Rebecca from down the street! I saw her!"

I slid farther into the crowd.

"Rebecca?" The officer scanned the people, then spotted me. "Rebecca, come here."

I sighed. "I'm here." I began to edge closer. Finally, I again stood beside Kris. "I'm here," I repeated.

"Did you see this young man tear this off the gatepost?"

I looked at Kris.

He was smiling slightly. He looked at me, raised his eyebrows, and nodded slightly.

I turned back to the officer. "Umm . . . yes, I did," I said.

"That's good enough for me!" Mrs. Schmidt said loudly.

"For me too," the officer said. "I'm afraid you'll have to come with me, son," he said, putting a hand on Kris's shoulder. The two of them disappeared into the crowd, the officer clutching the telltale board in one hand and Kris in the other.

The crowd quickly dispersed.

I was watching the group of Elves. They had quietly turned and were walking down the street behind the officer and his prisoner.

CHAPTER TWO

I didn't hear anything more about Kris for six years.

For the first few months, I pestered Abel constantly about his cousin, but Abel was less than talkative on the subject of his law-breaking relative.

Finally, I stopped asking, though it didn't stop me from thinking about the tall boy with the magnetic blue eyes from Germany.

One hot, summer day, a group of us were sitting on Bert's lawn, sipping cool sassafras and talking, while we watched a group of four Elves making repairs to our street.

Because they were Elves and not trusted with any of the horses, they had to do the heavy work themselves and were obviously struggling.

I could see the moisture pouring off their small, wrinkled faces.

A large man in a sweaty, white shirt was in charge of

this particular street crew, and he didn't hesitate to let the whole block know it. His language and manner of speaking were both loud and obnoxious.

After one particularly ribald diatribe, Abel stood up. "Sir, it's nothing to me how you treat the Dienes in your life," he said, calmly, "but I'd like to remind you that there are ladies present."

The big man looked at Abel, then glanced at the rest of us. His face turned an even livelier shade of red and he mumbled something in which "please" was the only word decipherable.

Abel nodded at him, then turned to me. "Boy, I hope that doesn't happen when Kris gets here!"

My heart stopped. "Kris is coming here?"

"Yes."

"For a visit?"

"No."

"C'mon, Abel, what's the story?" Bert said. Never patient in the first place, he had obviously gotten tired of the noncommittal answers. He handed his glass to his hovering Elfa and got to his enormous feet.

Bert still tried to rule our little community. Based on size, alone, he probably could have done it. He stood several inches taller than any of the rest of us.

And quite a few pounds heavier.

But fortunately his intellect wouldn't allow it, being,

as it was, only a couple of points above the Stoltzes' cat.

And he had yet to out-wrestle me, the shortest in our group.

He ran a hand through his curly, red hair and turned slightly bulging eyes on Abel.

"So?"

Abel sighed. "Apparently, Kris's mother is having a difficult time meeting her obligations, being the sole breadwinner as she is."

"But what has that to do with us?" Bert leaned forward, putting his wide, red face close to Abel.

"Ugh, Bert. Back off, will you? Your breath smells like a pigsty!"

"That's cause that's where he lives!" Margaret said, flipping a long blonde lock behind one slender shoulder. "In a pigsty."

Bert glared at her. "Don't live in no *Diene* house!" he spat.

Margaret merely laughed.

Bert swung back to Abel. "So?"

Abel frowned and looked away. "His mama and my mama are sisters. Mama says that family doesn't let family starve. So we get to put up with them. Forever."

"Oh, great. There goes the neighborhood," Bert said.

"Oh, it won't be so bad," I said, watching the four sweating Elves. "Besides, maybe he had a point."

Everyone stared at me.

"You're not making sense, girl," Abel said.

I shrugged, turning again to watch the small Elves with their enormous task. And more enormous taskmaster.

Abel got up and stretched his tall, lean length. "Watching those Elves is making me hot. And tired." He pushed his dark hair back from his forehead. "I have to help Mama anyways," he said.

He started up the street.

"Anything I can help with?" I said.

He glanced over one shoulder. "Oh we're just, you know, making beds and stuff."

"Well, I don't know a lot about beds, but I use one," I said, getting to my feet. "I think I'll go and have a talk with your mama."

He shrugged but waited until I had joined him, and then he resumed his slow saunter toward his house.

"So when do they get here?"

"Oh. Today. Tomorrow. The next day. I'm not sure."

"Oh."

"They refuse to use Elf labour, so they have to do everything themselves. It's really hard to estimate how long things are going to take."

"Oh," I said again, frowning. "No Elf labour at all?"

Abel looked at me and raised his eyebrows.

"Huh." I tried to picture it. Getting out of bed and tidying my room. Making meals. Cleaning. I made a face.

Abel had been watching me. He chuckled and turned away. "Exactly," he said.

We were silent as we continued toward his house.

Abel's mother, Grace, was standing in the front yard. She was a small, slender woman with her son's dark hair and thin face. "Hello, Becca, dear," she said. "Hi, son."

Abel swept her into a big hug, lifting her off the ground. "Ahh! Abel, you're a beast!" she said, gasping.

Her son set her down and grinned.

"So what needs to be done, Mama?" he asked.

"Oh, the Dienes have pretty much finished," his mother said. "I've just come out here for a breath of fresh air and to see if there are any flowers suitable for a nice bouquet."

"I came to offer to . . . umm . . . help make beds," I said.

She smiled at me. "Well, that's wonderful, dear, but the Elves have things ready. Won't you come in for a cool drink?"

I found my eyes on the hard-working crew down the street. Quite suddenly, I wondered if anyone had ever offered any of those Elves a cool drink.

I shook my head and frowned. Weird. Where did that thought come from?

I rushed into speech. "Oh, thank you, Mrs. Bauer," I said, rather breathlessly, "but Abel and I just finished a drink over at Bert's."

She glanced over my shoulder. "Looks like they're still there."

I turned and looked at the group still seated on Bert's family's wide front lawn.

"Yes. They'll probably . . ." I got no further.

A wagon, pulled by a single horse and carrying two people, turned the corner and started toward us from up the street.

It was an ancient wagon. Drawn by an equally ancient mare.

"Oh, they're here!" Abel said.

"That's a relief," his mother said.

The wagon drew up to the curb.

"Hold up, Pet!" said the tall, blond young man holding the reins.

The single horse stopped immediately.

The young man jumped down and walked to the animal. Reaching it, he stroked and caressed its head and neck.

"Oh, who's a good girl? Pet's a good girl to do all of that hard work in this heat! Yes, you are!"

The horse nuzzled him, lipping the blond hair gently.

The three of us on the lawn stared at him.

Finally, he turned and walked back to the wagon.

After helping a small, slender woman alight, he grabbed a couple of cases from the wagon bed.

Finally he turned toward us and I saw those blue eyes.

Here indeed was the same young man who had broken Mrs. Schmidt's measurer all those years ago.

He followed his mother to the gate, pausing beside the Bauer's measurer for a moment before continuing on.

When he reached us, he had a smile pasted on his face, but I sensed that it hid his true feelings.

His mother and Abel's mother were hugging each other.

"Oh, Grace, I'm so grateful!" Kris's mother was saying, tearfully.

"Nonsense, Sissy!" Abel's mama said. "Family helps family! We're just so glad you made it safely!"

"Well, with Kris at the reins, absolutely nothing could go wrong," Sissy said, smiling proudly up at her son.

"Come over here and let me have a look at you, Kris!" Mrs. Bauer said.

Obediently, Kris dropped the two cases he held and moved to stand in front of her.

"Well, your mother hasn't been stinting on the food, I see," Mrs. Bauer said, smiling. She hugged him. "It's so good to have you here, son," she said softly.

"You probably remember Rebecca, right, Kris?" Abel said.

Kris released Mrs. Bauer and turned toward me.

"Ah! My partner in crime," he said, grinning. He held out his hand.

I felt my eyes widen. I shook his proffered hand briefly, then dropped it fast.

"And this is Kris's mother, Mrs. Kringle," Abel said. He looked at her. "This is my friend Rebecca," he said.

I turned to the slight woman.

"Hello, dear," she said softly, holding out her arms for a hug.

I leaned forward uncomfortably and felt her arms close around me.

I was pleasantly surprised. It felt . . . nice.

Reluctantly, I moved away and her hands dropped.

"Well, why don't you all go inside and rest," Kris said. "I'll take care of Pet and join you in a moment."

"I'll help you," Abel said.

"And me!" I joined them.

Kris took the lead rein and the three of us walked beside the ancient mare and her wagon up the drive and around to the stable in the back.

Two Elves greeted us politely from the stable's door.

"Masters. Mistress," one of them said, bowing respectfully.

"Diene, I want you to take care of the horse," Abel directed. "Make her comfortable."

"Never mind . . . er . . . what's your name? Your *real* name," Kris said to the Elf who had spoken.

I gasped. Never was an Elf called by his or her real name. We called them all "Diene." Because . . . well, because.

"Hank, master," the Elf said, frowning.

"Well, Hank," Kris said. "I'll look after my own horse. But I'd love the company!"

Hank and his companion looked at each other, then followed Kris uncertainly into the shadowy barn.

Abel and I also exchanged a glance. Abel's eyebrows were raised. I shook my head and moved into the barn.

It was spotlessly clean. Abel's Elves were obviously good at what they did. Better, even, than ours.

For the next quarter of an hour, I sat on a pile of hay in a corner and watched as the two boys and the two Elves found a spot for Pet and got her and the wagon settled.

In that time, I got a glimpse of the man Kris had become.

"So tell me about your family, Hank," Kris said as he brushed Pet vigorously.

At first, the Elves were a bit slow to respond. I guessed they weren't as accustomed to conversation as we were.

"Well, there's my wife, Betta," Hank said softly. "And we have four Elfas and two Elfs."

"Wow. Six kids. That must keep you hopping!"

"It truly does," Hank agreed.

"So are they in school or what?"

"Yes. They all go to school," Hank said. "They are at the top of their classes!"

"So where does your family live?"

"Oh, we are luckier than most. We have a house!"

"Really!" Kris glanced at Abel and I, his face pinched momentarily in a tight frown. "A whole house!"

"Well, not a whole house," Hank was quick to clarify. "We have two rooms. But we are very comfortable."

"Huh." Kris finished brushing the horse and backed out of her stall. He tossed the brush into a bin and closed the lid. Then he rubbed his hands together. "There. That's that," he said. "Now, where do I find the feed?"

"Oh, we can do that for you!" Hank said eagerly. "Please."

"Well, I still need to know where everything is, so if you'd direct me . . ."

Hank trotted along beside Kris, chattering happily as they moved to the far end of the huge building.

I looked at Abel, and we exchanged another glance.

"Did you know that . . . ummm . . . *Hank* had a family?" I whispered to him.

"Are you kidding?" Abel said. "I don't think I've exchanged two words with the Elf since we hired him! But I figured he must have. Elves breed like rabbits!"

The other Elf glanced at us, then grabbed a large, tin bucket and ran outside with it. Soon, we heard the sound of the pump in the yard.

In moments, the Elf was back, carrying the bucket now brimming with clear water.

He fastened it to the wall of Pet's stall and gave the old horse a gentle pat.

"Please, Master Kris, let me do that!"

Kris and Hank had reappeared. Kris had an armful of hay under one arm, and a bucket of grain in the other hand.

"No, Hank, if I give you all of the work, I'll just grow fat and lazy."

Hank laughed a high-pitched little giggle. "But, Master Kris, if you don't let me help, then *I'll* grow fat and lazy!"

Kris tipped his head and looked down at his companion. He appeared to consider this remark. "Well, if

you insist," he said finally. "If we share the work, then maybe we'll each only get mildly fat."

"And mildly lazy!" Hank said.

They both laughed—Kris's a rich baritone, the Elf's a high treble.

Kris handed the Elf the bucket.

"Well, I've seen enough," Abel said. "Come on, Becca. Let's get out of here."

"Wait. Kris is almost done," I said.

Kris dropped the hay he was carrying into the manger in Pet's stall.

Hank emptied the bucket into a clean, wooden box, then laughed again as the large horse tried to shove him aside to get at the grain.

"Pet, my dear, your manners leave much to be desired," he said.

Pet snorted and dipped her soft nose into her feed.

The Elf and the man watched her for a moment.

Then Hank turned to Kris. "Don't worry, Master Kris, we'll take good care of your friend."

"Thank you, Hank." Kris dropped a large hand on the small shoulder. "I know you will."

"Can we go now?" Abel said.

Kris smiled. "Certainly!" He followed us out into the sunshine.

We found the two sisters sitting up on the shady

terrace, glasses of cool liquid in their hands.

Abel's Elfa was standing near them, pouring out three more.

She smiled as she handed one of them to me.

"Thank you, Diene," I said, taking it and finding a chair near the other two women.

"Oh, you're a lifesaver," Kris said as he reached for another glass. He downed his drink in one gulp and reached for the pitcher.

"Please allow me to pour, Master," the Elfa said softly.

"Come now, a gentleman never allows a lady to serve him," Kris said.

"A lady . . ." She gave a little nervous half-giggle and glanced at Mrs. Bauer, who was looking at them, a slight frown between her brows.

Kris pulled the crystal pitcher from the small hands and proceeded to pour himself a drink. He carried it over to the chair next to mine and sank into it gratefully.

"Ah, this is great!" he said, closing his eyes and stretching out long legs in front of him.

He took another swallow and leaned his head back against the seat.

Finally, he opened his eyes to find the rest of us staring at him.

"What?" he said.

"Kris, I think we need to have a talk," Abel said.

CHAPTER THREE

*O*ver the next few weeks, Kris became known as the crackpot who treated Elves as though they were equals.

It got him into several . . . uncomfortable situations. Which he seemed to weather quite well.

Living next door as he now did, he and I had numerous opportunities to talk, many of which, I had begun to suspect, he had sought out.

So he also became my friend.

Several weeks into the summer, I was in our front yard, clipping some flowers for a bouquet for the front hall.

There was a conversation going on next door that I could hear a little too clearly.

"Kris, what have you done?" Mr. Bauer's unmistakable roar.

"Removed your measurer."

"But . . . why?"

I moved slowly down toward the street until I had a

clear view of the two men standing outside the Bauer's front gate.

Kris was holding a white painted board.

I was struck forcibly with a distinct sense of déjà vu.

"Because I don't like it," Kris said. "I find it offensive."

"Offensive? How?"

Kris took a deep breath and let it out slowly. "Doesn't it bother you that thinking, talented persons are being treated like slaves in your community?"

"Now, son, you simply don't understand—"

But Kris broke in. "Don't understand? What's to understand? These are talented, wonderful, *loving*, living beings who should be treated with at least the same respect we give to all other creatures."

"Now, son, they simply don't feel things the same way we do."

"What? Are you listening to yourself? Those 'creatures' have hopes and dreams. They feel pain and hunger and joy. They marry and have families and care for their children."

"Yes, yes. Much the same as our horses," Mr. Bauer said. "Well, except for the 'marrying' thing."

"And that one thing should tell you everything!"

Mr. Bauer shook his head. "I'll let this go for now," he said. "You're new here, and you don't understand how we do things." He turned and walked up the drive.

"I hope I never 'understand,'" Kris said softly.

"Hello, Kris!" I said. "Rocking the boat?"

He looked up, then snorted softly and nodded. "Yeah. Just like always."

He turned and flopped down on the grass beside the fence, his head sunk dejectedly between his shoulders.

Ignoring the new frock I had put on with such anticipation only a few minutes before, I sat beside him.

"Kris, some things you just have to go along with," I said.

He raised his head and looked piercingly at me. "No, Becca. Some things you never have to 'go along' with," he said.

"But all it will do is cause problems."

He dropped his head once more. "I can handle problems."

I was silent for a moment. "But what about your mama, Kris. What does this do to her?"

He sighed. "That's my only concern," he said softly. He leaned his head back against the fence. "I remember the first time I saw one of those blasted 'measurers,'" he said. "It was right here on this street."

"I remember," I said.

"Over there."

The two of us glanced up the street toward Mrs. Schmidt's house.

"I remember that too."

He smiled crookedly, then sobered once more. "I couldn't believe that anyone . . . any *thinking* person . . . could do that to another thinking person."

"Well, most people don't think of the Elves as 'persons,'" I pointed out.

"Yeah, don't I know it!" He rubbed his eyes with one hand. "Anyway, it wasn't long after that . . . encounter . . . with Mrs. Schmidt, that someone introduced your *wonderful* custom into our city."

"Really?"

"Yes. I remember the first time I saw one in my own community. I wanted to tear it off its post . . ."

"Like you did here."

"Well, yes." Again that half-smile. "I did."

"Did what?"

"Tore it off the post."

"Oh, Kris!" I said sadly.

He shrugged. "I tore a lot of them off. Spent a lot of time in the detention hall. But people just kept putting them back up." He looked at me. "It isn't the measurers themselves, but what they represent that I resent," he said. "The subjugation of another group."

"Sub . . . what?"

He smiled again. "Subjugation. It means suppression, for the tiny minds in our midst."

I folded my arms and glared at him.

"Anyway, it finally became too hard."

"I can imagine how hard it must have been for you," I said in my most soothing voice.

He snorted. "Not me. I mean for my mama. We were asked to leave."

"They asked you to leave?"

"Well, *demanded* would be a more accurate term. Their actual words were 'desist or depart.'"

"Poetic."

He scowled.

"Kris. Why didn't you just . . . stop?"

He looked at me, disgusted. "Becca, this is *me* we're talking about."

"What was I thinking?" I said, shaking my head.

"It was so difficult for my mama," he said. "Having to leave her home. But everything had gotten so bad for her. It was only because of her that I consented. We packed up, sold off, and left."

"You feel that strongly about this?"

"Becca, we should all feel that strongly about this!"

He then jumped to his feet. "Come with me," he said, holding out his hand.

I stared at his hand. "What?"

"I want to show you something."

"Alone?"

He made a face at me. "Becca, what do you think I'm going to do?"

I gave him my hand. "Oh, I'm not worried about you. It's just . . . what will everyone say if I go off with you and no chaperone?"

"Like we care what others may think!" he scoffed as he helped me to my feet.

"I care!" I said hotly. "I have to live here!"

He smiled his soft, gentle smile. "I live here too, Becca," he said, quietly.

"But you don't . . . you . . ." I was lost for words.

His smiled widened. "Exactly!" he said, starting up the street. He glanced back at me. "Coming?"

I scratched my head and looked around. Then I glanced down at the light, leather slippers on my feet, hardly the footwear for a long walk.

I looked again at Kris. "Is it far?"

"Not physically." His eyes were sparkling eagerly. "But leagues culturally."

"I don't know what you are talking about."

He laughed. "I know. But you will. Coming?"

"I guess so," I said finally, falling into step with him.

The two of us walked across town, passing through neighborhood after neighborhood.

It was an education for me.

Oh, I had crossed town before but always in our

family's carriage. And I had never really noticed that the farther we moved from my neighborhood, the smaller and more closely packed the homes grew.

Finally, we came to the bridge spanning the river.

I stopped. "I'm not supposed to cross the river, Kris," I said.

"Why ever not?" he asked.

"Papa told me that things are uncivilized on the other side of the bridge."

"Uncivilized?" Kris snorted softly. "Well, they are uncivilized on one side of the bridge, that's for certain."

"So we shouldn't go."

"No, we *should* go." He smiled. "I was talking about *your* side of the river."

"*Our* side is the uncivilized side?"

He grinned. "That's what I'm saying."

"I'm going home." I turned.

"Wait, Becca! Please."

I hesitated.

"Please let me show you. I promise you'll be safe."

I turned back and looked at him. "Safe?"

"I promise."

I shrugged. "You had better be telling the truth."

"I am," he said. He took my hand and started across the bridge.

Just on the other side, the grass was green and slightly

overgrown. A flock of sheep was grazing a short distance away, where the forest started. From their enthusiasm, they had just been turned into this fresh pasture.

Kris led me to a worn track that wound through the trees. I regarded it suspiciously, then glanced once more at my slippers. I sighed audibly and Kris turned to look at me.

"Still scared?"

"No . . . that is . . . no," I said. "I just don't think my shoes are up to the challenge." I lifted my skirt just far enough to stick out one foot. I wiggled my toes.

Kris looked at the slipper and grinned. "Don't worry, Becca," he said. "This track is just dirt. Smooth and soft."

"You'd better be right," I said, raising my eyebrows at him.

He laughed.

We started to follow the track and soon the forest closed over us.

It was cool and green under the trees. Birds were making an enormous amount of cheerful noise, and I found myself relaxing.

This was peaceful.

Then I stepped on something hard. "Ouch!"

Kris stopped. "What's the matter?"

I hopped up and down on one foot as I cradled my abused foot in my hand. "I stepped on something!"

"Oh. Sorry," he said, grinning.

"Is that all you can say?" I glared at him.

"Becs, I'm really sorry!" He continued to grin.

"Why do I trust you?" I asked. "Here you are with your heavy boots. How could you possibly know if the track is rocky or not!"

He frowned and looked at the track. "Huh. I guess you're right. Well, come on."

"What? I'm not going any further!"

"Come on, Becs. You'll really like it."

"My foot hurts." I held it out for him to see.

He walked over and frowned at my foot. Then, suddenly, he reached out and picked me up.

"Kris! What are you doing?"

He laughed. "Helping a lady in distress."

"Kris!" I began to struggle.

He merely tightened his grip and continued on.

"Kris . . . Kris . . ."

"Yes? Yes?"

"Oh, you're impossible!"

He grinned again. "I know!" He seemed to stumble and gave a sudden dip.

I shrieked and threw my arms around his neck.

His grin widened.

"You did that on purpose!"

"You're right. And it worked too!"

We continued on, Kris holding me. And me with my arms wrapped around his neck.

I realized that I was enjoying myself. It must have been because I was tired of walking. And I obviously wasn't accustomed to so much exercise because my heart was pounding. At least I told myself it was from the exercise . . .

The track twisted back and forth, then opened suddenly out into a meadow.

Kris stopped and gently set me on my feet.

I stared.

Before me was an entire little village. A neat, single street of hard-packed dirt was lined with cute little cottages and shops, all of them scrupulously clean and cared for.

Tiny offspring ran and played happily. Adults hurried about busily or stood, talking in groups.

It was a peaceful, prosperous scene. And it was peopled entirely by Elves.

I blinked.

Kris continued forward. He looked over his shoulder. "Coming?" he said.

"It's Kris!" a high-pitched voice sang out.

"Oh-oh, we've been spotted," he said, grinning. "No backing out now."

Immediately, we were surrounded by tiny,

dark-haired Elf children, all similarly dressed in tunics and trousers and small, pointed shoes in the greens and reds and browns of the forest.

They jumped and hopped excitedly around Kris. Many small hands reached out to touch or pat him.

I tried to stay close to him, but I was finding it increasingly difficult as the little Elves jostled each other and me for a position nearest their hero.

"Master Kris!" a larger, only slightly deeper voice called out.

I looked up just as several figures detached themselves from a group and headed toward us.

This time, I managed to move closer to him and heard his deep chuckle.

"They don't bite, Becs," he whispered, grinning at me.

"Master Kris!" said the same voice once again.

Or maybe it was a different one.

I had difficulty telling one from another.

The group joined us.

"Shoo, my littles," one of them said, chuckling.

The children scattered, laughing shrilly.

Each of the little Elf men reached out with eager hands to shake Kris' rather large one.

"We're so glad you're here, Master Kris," the same Elf spoke. "Did you hear?"

"I've just come for an overdue visit," Kris said. "Hear what?"

"My daughter, Sophie, is getting ready to have her baby!"

"Oh, Niklas, that *is* good news!" Kris said, smiling.

I stared at the small speaker in horror. Someone was having a baby? And they were discussing it? Openly?

I was right. Elves were completely uncivilized.

"Umm . . . Kris, we'd better go," I whispered.

He looked at me. "Why?"

I stared at him. "A lady doesn't . . . a lady . . ."

He chuckled. "A lady doesn't bear babies?"

I frowned at him and stamped my uninjured foot. "Of course not!"

"Well, then, where do their babies come from?"

"Oh, you are impossible! I meant . . . that's not what I meant! Of course they have babies! They just aren't supposed to . . . talk about it." I looked around. I could feel my face getting warm. "At least not in . . . company."

"Well, that's just silly," Kris said, dismissing me.

I felt my jaw drop open as I stared at him.

"Close you mouth, Becs," he said, without turning. "You look funny."

I snapped it shut and glared at him. Then I straightened and, turning, began to march indignantly in the direction of home.

"Better not do it, Becs," he said softly. "You never know what you will meet out there in the woods."

I stopped instantly and scrambled back to the safety of his large presence.

Then I grabbed his sleeve.

He chuckled again and led me further into the village. "Well, I wouldn't miss this for the world!" he said loudly. "We'd better find a spot to wait."

"Oh, come with me, Kris," one of the Elves said. "I have a very comfortable place."

Kris nodded and indicated that the Elf should lead on.

We were directed to the largest structure in the entire village. A barn.

"Oh, this is nice," Kris said, disappearing inside.

I stood in the doorway and peered suspiciously into the dim interior, then sniffed. Mounds of fresh, dried grasses.

But . . . a barn.

"Kris, I don't think I should . . ." I began.

"Oh, come on, Becs," he said. "There's nothing wrong with resting here for a while."

"Are you mad?" I said, incredulous. "Going into a barn with you, unchaperoned, is already way up on the 'never do' list. Then add to that 'lying down in the hay' and 'being alone.' I can't tell you the number of rules I am breaking just by being here. Let's not make it worse than it is!"

He shook his head. "Ah, Becs. When will you learn that what other people think doesn't matter? All that is really important is what we think of ourselves."

I lifted my nose into the air. "Well, if *I* haven't learned that in nearly sixteen years of life, perhaps it really isn't correct," I said.

He laughed. "If you haven't learned that in nearly sixteen years, it just means that you've had faulty tutors."

I turned from the barn.

A short distance away, I spied a little stool. Walking over, I picked it up. It seemed a sturdy, solid little thing. I carried it back and parked it beside the doorway. Then I sat down and leaned back against the sun-warmed wood to wait.

I could hear the murmur of voices from inside the barn. The higher pitch of Elf voices and the lower pitch that could only be Kris.

I moved my stool closer to the open door.

"So we've been waiting a long time for this," one of the Elves was saying.

"I'm so happy for them," Kris said. "And for you. This is a momentous occasion on so many levels."

"It really is," the Elf said. "It's wonderful to know that the line will go on."

"Well, there are many capable Elves who could carry on," Kris said.

"Oh, that is true," the Elf replied. "But my people are resistant to change. They have had me as their leader for so long that they simply can't conceive of anyone else, regardless of how long they've known him."

"Or her." I could hear the smile in Kris's voice.

"Or her," the Elf said.

"Well, this new baby will signal the continuation of your line, finally."

"How do you spell *relief*?" the Elf said. "B-A-B-Y!"

Kris laughed.

My stool was getting distinctly uncomfortable.

I shifted around a bit, trying to find a better position.

"Stool too small?" a voice asked.

I turned. An Elfa was standing at the corner of the barn, watching me.

"It is," I said. "Do you have anything larger?"

The Elfa shook her head. "Sorry," she said.

I shifted again. "Don't you anticipate needing larger things for larger people?" I said.

She tipped her head to one side. "No," she said. "The Big Ones never come here. Well, unless they are looking for laborers or someone to blame for something."

"Well, don't they need someplace to sit?"

"Oh, they're never here long enough for that," the

little Elfa said. "They take what they want and leave."

"Oh." What did one say to that? I shifted again.

"Not fun to be forced to use something not quite your size, is it?" the Elfa said.

"No, it isn't!" I said, rather crossly. It was getting hot out here in the sun. And parts of me were really starting to get . . . uncomfortable.

"Yes. We Elves completely understand that."

I stared at her with narrowed, suspicious eyes, but she returned my gaze blandly.

Then she nodded at me and disappeared around the corner.

There was a sudden stirring in the group of Elves across the street. One of them was pointing and saying something excitedly.

I could hear the sound of the high, little voice, but I couldn't make out the words.

Then I saw another Elf running toward them.

The figure grew closer. I could see long skirts flipping and twisting around the small, booted feet. Ah, another Elfa.

"Midwife!" someone shouted.

The midwife skidded to a halt in the center of the group and said something in a quick high-pitched voice.

Several of the Elves pointed toward the barn.

The midwife nodded and, picking up her skirts, ran toward me.

"What is it, Beate?" One of the Elves had left the barn and was now standing next to me in the sunshine.

I jumped and turned my head, nearly falling from my uncomfortable perch.

"There's a problem, High Elf," the Elfa said. "With your daughter."

She spun around and headed back up the street with the Elf right behind her. The two disappeared into one of the tiny homes at the far end of the village.

"I hope everything will be all right," Kris's voice spoke up from beside me.

I jumped again and, this time, lost my balance on my tiny stool. With a squeak of alarm, I landed in the dirt.

"Oh, sorry, Becs," Kris said, giving me a hand up. "Didn't mean to startle you."

"Everything here startles me," I said testily, brushing at my frock. "I'm already nervous to begin with, and then people keep appearing out of nowhere."

"People?"

"Well, Elves."

"Oh. I was wondering . . ." He cleared his throat. "Never mind."

"So what's happening?" I said.

Kris looked down the street. "I don't know," he said. "But I'm worried."

"Worried? About Elves?" My voice raised, incredulously.

The street went silent, and I felt everyone's eyes on me.

Kris sighed. "Yes, Becs. Worried. About Elves. This little one has been anticipated for a very long time." He glanced around.

The groups had stopped staring at us and were resuming their interrupted conversations.

"The Elfa waiting to deliver is the only daughter of this town's leader. Her baby will one day lead these people."

The Elf who had followed the midwife reappeared. He walked quickly to the center of the street.

"Please gather 'round me, my brothers and sisters," he said.

The other Elves immediately moved toward him.

He was silent for a few moments. Then he took a deep breath. "There is a problem," he said. "Things are not proceeding as they should." He paused and, pulling a large, green cloth from a back pocket, proceeded to mop at his leathery, lined face.

It was then that I realized that the old Elf was crying. Crying.

I frowned.

He blew his nose. "We need . . . help," he said.

The crowd was silent. All eyes were on their leader. Even the tiny children were watching.

He cleared the huskiness from his throat. "I need you to pray with me," he said.

"C'mon, Becs," Kris said. "Let's join them."

"What?" I said. "But . . . but . . ."

"Eloquent as always, my dear," he said, smiling. "Come on."

He took my arm and towed me to the edge of the crowd.

The High Elf saw us and nodded at Kris and smiled briefly.

Then he bowed his head.

The rest of the village did the same.

"Father Creator," he paused. Then he took a deep breath and began again. "Father, we thank you for our . . . blessings," he said. "We recognize your guidance and your help and your strengthening influence in our lives. But we need you now . . ." His voice broke and he was silent for a moment. Then, finally, "We have a small spirit waiting to join us. We have been waiting for this little one for a very long time. You know, Father, what the birth of this baby will mean to this community. Will you please help us now? Help this little one. Strengthen and bless the mother and father. And please, Father, strengthen and bless this baby. Please bring her to us safely. But, Father Creator," his voice sank to a whisper, "as always, we bow to your greater knowledge. Amen."

There was an answering echo of "Amens" and the Elves lifted their heads.

Odd. They all looked . . . relieved.

I thought of the prayers uttered by the pastor of our church. Fine prayers. Fancy prayers.

But never had they affected me as much as this Elf's simple words had done.

"Here," Kris was holding a clean, white kerchief in front of me. "You might need this."

It was then that I realized that I had tears streaming down my cheeks. Good heavens! What on earth was wrong with me?

These were Elves!

They weren't . . . human!

I watched as an Elfa reached for a small child near her and gathered it close. The child nestled against her, rubbed a little nose on her sleeve, and then darted away to resume play.

She smiled as she watched it go.

I looked around. Other members of the group were also gathering their little ones close for a hug, then letting them run.

The High Elf had disappeared once more.

"Well, back to the barn," Kris said, taking my arm.

CHAPTER FOUR

This time, I followed him into the cool interior and found a comfortable seat on a mound of hay next to the wall.

I sank down gratefully.

"Now, isn't this better?" he said.

"You'd better not tell my mama," I said. "She'll never let me talk to you again!"

I had meant it to be a jest, but Kris frowned sharply at my words.

I was instantly apologetic.

"I'm sorry Kris. I didn't mean it."

"I know, Becs," he said softly. "But, let's just say, it wouldn't be the first time that something like that happened."

"What? That people wouldn't let their kids talk to you?"

"Or even acknowledge me."

"I'm so sorry, Kris."

He shrugged. "It's a path I've chosen," he said. "It's just that . . . sometimes, it's a lonely path."

I looked at him.

He lay back in the hay and stared up at the beams of the roof high above our heads.

"Why do you do it, Kris?"

He smiled crookedly. "Why do I make such a nuisance of myself?"

I smiled too. "Well, yes."

"It's because of my father," he said.

"I thought he had . . . died."

"Well, it's how he died." He looked at me. "Do you mind if I tell you? It might help you to understand my peculiar perspective."

"No. I mean, yes, please, I'd like to hear it."

He was silent for a moment. "It was a very wet year."

"Rainy?"

"More rain than we had had in a generation," he said. "Perhaps ever. The rivers, streams, and lakes were all swollen to capacity, and, in some places, more than capacity. Low lying areas were being evacuated in anticipation of more rain and possible flooding."

He looked at me. "You probably didn't know it, but my father was a local landowner. His holdings were quite large and he had many, many families of Elves who worked their own little pieces of it.

"Anyway, as any good landowner should, he was out with his men, checking to make sure that everyone was safe, Elves and humans and animals. He and his group were riding back toward the manor when it struck."

"What struck?"

"A flash flood. It had been raining heavily all day, and they were crossing what was normally a small creek bed. It was already high on its banks, but they figured it wouldn't be too much trouble to cross. Several of the men were already on the far side, waiting for the rest of the group. Papa and one other man were right in the middle when the wall of water struck them, knocking their horses over and sending them down the creek.

"The other man managed to make his way to the edge and was pulled to safety, but they lost sight of my father almost immediately.

"Several of the men rode downstream along the banks, trying to catch sight of him, but to no avail.

"They searched for hours, but finally had to call it off because of the treacherous conditions as darkness fell. By that point, they figured that he was probably dead and told my mother and I so.

"But we found out later, he hadn't died immediately. Instead, he had been washed downstream to a small settlement of Elves. Someone there spotted him in the water, and they immediately stopped what they were doing and charged into the mad waters to rescue him."

Kris was silent for so long that I turned to look at him again. He was, once more, staring up at the ceiling.

He took a deep breath. "They didn't succeed, and three of them gave their lives trying.

"I'll never forget it. The pouring rain. The mud-caked wagons. The silent, shrouded figures within. And the obvious sorrow of the quietly sobbing Elves. And the most touching thing was that they were trying, in their grief, to comfort my mama and I."

Kris took another rather shaky breath. "I had always known that they were beings of extraordinary gifts and talents, but it was then that I recognized the depth of feeling they were capable of.

"From then on, they did everything they could to help my mama and I. They instructed her in directing the affairs of our family holdings. Schooled me in the duties of animal husbandry and the myriad tasks that were farming.

"But one thing they didn't understand—the law. And it was through those legal channels, ably followed by cunning men, that Mama and I were finally squeezed from our lands and home."

"Oh, Kris!"

He shook his head. "It's all right. We were . . . compensated . . . and were able to purchase a comfortable home in the nearest town. But Mama never got over the fact that she hadn't been able to save Papa's legacy."

"But, Kris, it wasn't her fault!" I said.

"She knows that. But knowing it and *knowing it* are two separate things."

I sat quietly, thinking about what Kris had said.

He sat up suddenly, looking toward the door, and it was then I realized that the noise level outside had increased.

Just then, a figure appeared.

"Master Kris, she's come!"

"Thank the Father!" Kris said. He jumped to his feet and charged toward the doorway.

I was right behind him.

A crowd had gathered outside the house up the street, and they were cheering and shouting excitedly.

"That baby's going to be sorry she left her nice, quiet nest," Kris said, laughing.

I joined him.

We were soon surrounded by Elves, all singing and shouting for joy.

What a difference from only an hour before, I thought.

"Come, Master Kris, my Lady. You must join us in a muggins!" The High Elf had joined us, carrying a tiny, blanket-wrapped bundle. "See! See her? Isn't she the most precious thing you ever saw?" He moved the

blanket aside, and I caught a glimpse of an alert, wide-eyed baby. It was calmly, even curiously, surveying the world from night-dark eyes.

The High Elf handed the baby to another Elf who had been hovering closely. "Here, Papa, hold your daughter!" he said.

The other Elf broke into a wide smile. "My daughter!" he said loudly.

Everyone cheered.

And quite suddenly, I found a small, heavy mug pressed into my hand.

"A toast! A toast! A muggins to our new daughter!" The High Elf lifted a similar glass and drank deeply of its contents.

"Go ahead, Becs. Drink. It doesn't get any better than this!"

I watched Kris lift his cup to his lips, then I did the same. The drink was, at once, tart and sweet and spicy. And absolutely delicious.

"Mmmm. Good," I said.

Kris' eyes twinkled. "I knew you'd like it!" he said. "It's called cider. The Elves make it. It's their specialty."

I drained my cup and looked around for more.

But Kris took the cup from my hand and gave it to an Elfa passing by with a tray.

"Better that we go now, dear," he said. "This

celebration is likely to go on for some time. Perhaps all night. These people love their babies, and this one has been especially anticipated."

He took my arm and led me from the tangle of small bodies.

"Master Kris! Wait!" The High Elf joined us just as we reached the trees.

Kris turned and smiled. "Congratulations, Niklas," he said, extending his hand.

The Elf smiled and shook it. "The best of days," he said.

"And many more in the future," Kris said.

The old Elf's smile disappeared for a moment. Then he took a deep breath and smiled once more. "Of course," he said simply.

"I just have one question, Niklas," Kris said. "How did you know it was going to be a girl?"

"What?"

"In your prayer, you prayed that *she* would arrive safely."

The old Elf smiled. "You noticed that, did you?"

"It was hard not to."

"Well, maybe that was just a lucky guess."

"Doubtful."

"Or a slip of the tongue."

"Even less likely."

He laughed, a high giggle of sound. "Well, let's just say, then, that it was a gift. Like the baby herself."

"Okay, I'll go along with that."

"Good-bye, my friend," the High Elf said. "Please come back soon!"

"I will," Kris said. "And thank you."

"And be sure to bring your lady friend with you!"

Kris looked at me and grinned. "Is that an order?"

"Most assuredly."

"Then consider it done."

The old Elf laughed again and turned back toward the village.

"Did he really mean that?" I said.

"You'll find that Elves never say anything they don't mean," Kris said. "They are transparently honest."

"Huh."

"That's all you can think of to say?"

"Yes. Huh."

He laughed.

The walk back was necessarily slow. My foot was still tender from the rock I had stepped on earlier, and I refused to let Kris carry me.

Finally, we reached the bridge.

I paused and looked back. In the few hours we

had spent there with the Elves, my attitude had made a complete adjustment. Before, the woods had meant something unknown and terrifying. Now, they seemed to breathe out peace and goodwill.

Strange.

Kris and I made our way back across town to our street. Several people were gathered in front of my home, talking excitedly.

Then one of them spotted us. "There she is!"

"Uh-oh," Kris said, grinning.

Everyone turned to look at us.

Then I saw my mama leave the group and make her way toward us.

"Uh-oh," I echoed.

Mama stopped a short distance away and put her hands on her hips. "Mary Rebecca Hahn, where have you been?" she asked.

"Kris and I just went for a walk," I said, limping toward her.

She broke in. "Are you limping? You're limping! What's the matter?" She closed the distance between us.

"Oh, it's nothing. I just stepped on a silly rock. That's why we took so long getting back."

"Oh." She paused and glanced at Kris, then reached out and put an arm around my shoulders. "Come along, child. Let's get you up to the house and have a look at it."

"Mama, I'm all right!" I said. "I can make it the rest of the way myself!"

Mama dropped her arm and glanced once more at Kris. "Well, thank you, Kris, for getting her back to us," she said briefly. "And don't mistake me. I think you're a fine boy, but you and I are going to have to have a talk soon about proper decorum. And chaperones!"

"I accept full blame, Mrs. Hahn," Kris said, bowing slightly. "I wanted to go for a walk, and I urged her to come with me. I can assure you that at no time was she in any danger."

Mama stared at him, then nodded briefly. "Well, we'll see," she said and turned away.

"Thanks for the walk, Kris," I said. "It was an . . . education."

He grinned at me. "Good," he said.

CHAPTER FIVE

That experience signalled a change in my life.

No longer was I able to dismiss the Elves as unimportant or unfeeling.

They had become "people" in my mind—caring, intelligent people, who deserved respect and affection.

My attitude couldn't help but be noticed.

"Thank you, Diene. That will be all." Papa dismissed our table attendant without looking up.

"Diene, what's the matter?" I asked.

She stopped dead. Then turned slowly toward me, her mouth a perfect circle of wonder in her wrinkled, brown face.

My parents too stopped what they were doing. Papa with a spoon raised halfway to his mouth.

"Why . . . w-what do you mean, Miss Rebecca?" Diene stammered.

"You keep rubbing your forehead. Do you have a headache?"

Diene glanced at my parents, still frozen in place. "Umm . . well, yes, Miss Rebecca."

"I want you to leave the rest of the serving to me and go and lie down," I said, getting to my feet. "Here. I'll get you a cool cloth. That should help."

I ushered the small woman into the kitchen, completely ignoring the gasps of both of my parents.

Our cook stopped in the act of removing a large roast from the hot oven and stared at us.

"Diene has a headache," I said.

The Elfa nodded uncertainly and resumed her task. I could see the perspiration running down the sides of her face as she bent over the hot oven.

I shook my head. This was August, in the hottest season of the year! And she was slaving, quite literally, over a broiling stove!

First things first.

"Let's get a cloth, shall we?" I stopped in the middle of the room. "Umm, okay, you'll have to help me just a bit, Diene. Where are the cloths?"

The Elfa moved dazedly toward one of the cupboards and opened it to reveal a neat stack of linens.

"Good. Now sit down."

"Oh, Miss Rebecca, I don't think I . . ."

"Sit!" I said.

She walked over to one of the kitchen chairs and

climbed up onto it, letting her feet dangle.

For a moment, I was reminded of the small stool I had perched on in the Elf village. And the words of the Elfa who had spoken to me.

Size did make a difference.

I scratched my head uncomfortably and tried to concentrate on what I was doing.

Walking to the sink, I pumped out clear, cold water and soaked the cloth. Wringing it out, I told Diene to lean her head back against the chair and let me lay the cloth across her brow.

The dark eyes regarded me uncertainly, but she obeyed.

"Ahh!" she said softly as I laid the cool cloth against the heated flesh.

Her eyes closed.

"Better?"

"Much," she said.

"Good. Now, Diene, what is the next course?"

"Agathe."

"Beg pardon?"

"My name is Agathe."

"Oh. Well, Agathe, what is the next course?"

I wasn't accustomed to the work, but I was a quick learner.

Over the next few months, I learned how to cook, sew, and clean. The cooking and sewing, I enjoyed.

The cleaning, not so much.

"Oh, Miss Rebecca! Here, let me help you with that!"

I was perched, rather precariously, atop a box atop a chair, trying to fasten the last of the crystal pendants to the parlour chandelier.

"It's okay, Agathe. I'm nearly finished."

"Oh, Miss Rebecca, you scared me!"

I looked down at the small upturned face, filled with anxiety.

Anxiety over me.

What creatures these Elves were. Mistreat them, even abuse them, and they kept on caring. They could teach us so much.

I shook my head and hooked the last pendant into place.

"There!" I dusted one hand against the other. And gasped as the box I stood on suddenly slipped out from under me.

"Oh!" Agathe squealed.

The box clattered to the floor, and I found myself sitting down, hard and rather abruptly, on the chair.

For a moment, I struggled to breathe.

"Oh, Miss Rebecca, are you all right?" Agathe rushed over to me.

"I'm fine, Agathe!" I gasped out. "I'm fine!"

I giggled as I glanced down at the box lying on its side on the floor. "It could have been much worse!"

"Oh, Miss Rebecca!" Agathe reached out and hugged me. "You gave me such a fright!"

"What's going on here?" My mama asked, coming into the room.

Agathe's arms dropped abruptly and she turned. "Oh, mistress! Miss Rebecca almost fell!"

Mama peered at me suspiciously. "Are you all right, dear?"

"I'm fine, Mama," I said. "The box I was standing on slipped, that's all. It made me sit down a little bit too hard."

"I don't even want to go into the reasons why you might be standing on a box," Mama said, rubbing her forehead. "Diene, please leave us."

Agathe bowed slightly, gave my arm a final pat, and left the room.

"Her name is Agathe, Mama. I've told you that before."

"She is a Diene, Rebecca. That is her title and designation. That is what she will be called in my house."

I bowed my head so Mama couldn't see the fire I knew was flashing in my eyes.

"So here's where my girls have gotten to." My father's voice preceded him into the room.

Mama looked up. "Were you looking for us, dear?" she asked.

"I was indeed," Papa said. "It's too nice a day to be cooped up in the house. We don't know how many beautiful days will be left with the coming of fall, so I've ordered a picnic supper to be served outside on the terrace. The Bauers are coming over to play some whist."

"Oh, that's lovely, dear."

"I'd better go change." I got to my feet.

"Wait, dear," Mama said. "We need to have a talk first."

I sighed and sank down once more.

"Did I interrupt something?" Papa asked.

"No. You really should be here anyway," Mama said. "I was about to have a talk with Mary Rebecca."

Papa sat down. "This sounds serious."

"It is," Mama said. She turned back to me. "I've let you have your head in this, dear," she said. "But enough is enough."

"What's the matter?" Papa asked.

"Your daughter has been helping the Dienes," Mama said.

"Well, I can't see anything wrong—"

"Rolf, think about it," Mama interrupted. "She's grubbing around all day, cooking, cleaning, and . . . endangering herself."

"Oh, Mama, I'm hardly endangering myself!" I said.

Mama glanced at me. "My point is that it's hardly appropriate for a young woman of your stature to be crawling around on hands and knees, scrubbing floors."

"Pfff. What stature?" I said. "I'm the shortest person on the whole street. In fact, I'm only a few inches taller than the Elves!"

Papa glanced at me sharply, then lowered his eyes.

"That's not what I meant and you know it," Mama said, rather sharply.

I looked down and bit my lip.

"There are certain *rules* that we are expected to follow," she went on. "Rules that make everyone's life more comfortable."

"Well, all of the human's lives, at any rate," I said.

"Please don't interrupt, dear," Mama said.

"Sorry."

"Rebecca, you have been born into privilege. And that carries certain . . ."

"Responsibilities?" I said.

"Yes. Exactly."

"I agree, Mama," I said. "I think it is our duty, as the privileged, to set an example. Of caring. And giving. And serving."

Mama shook her head. "I don't follow, dear."

"I think it is up to us, as the community leaders,

to show others how compassionate we can be. How well we can care for our community. And *all* of its members."

Mama had been nodding as I spoke. Then, she stopped and peered at me suspiciously.

"What are you saying, Rebecca?"

"That I think it's time that we stopped treating Elves as though they were something disgusting. Or dirty."

"But they—"

I interrupted her. "Mama, don't you dare say that they *are* disgusting or dirty! Can you think of one single incident when you have observed an Elf in any state other than perfectly groomed and clean? I mean, other than when they are being forced to grub around in the dirt, serving some human. And can you think of any time, *any time*, when you've seen one who's less than respectful?"

"Well, I . . . well, Ara's sister . . ."

"No, Mama. I mean you. Have *you* ever observed any disrespect or anger or surliness? Ever?"

Mama was silent for a moment. Finally she straightened and sighed. "No, dear, I haven't."

"Exactly. So your prejudices—because that is what they are—are simply that: prejudices. Unfounded. Taught. Learned."

I leaned forward and put a hand on Mama's shoulder. "I know that they seem strange to you," I said.

"They are short. They have little, high-pitched voices. They move around quickly."

Mama nodded.

"But, Mama, I've seen them with their children. I've heard them pray."

"Pray?" Mama puckered her forehead in a frown.

"Yes. They're every bit as faithful as . . . well . . . as we humans are."

Papa snorted. "Judging by some people on this street, that's not much to measure by," he said.

Mama folded her hands in her lap and frowned.

Papa was smiling at me, his eyes shining. "Well done, Becca," he said, softly.

"It's all fine talk about treating the Elves as people," Mama said, finally. "But we still have to live in this neighborhood!"

"Oh, I think we can manage to live here and treat our servants with a modicum of respect," Papa said, laughing.

A couple of days later, I was heading out to the stable when I heard Mama's voice through the kitchen window.

"Yes. All right, I think I can manage that," she was saying. "Okay, Die . . . um . . . *Gretta*, what do I do now? Oh my stars!"

I heard the sound of breaking crockery.

"Oh, dear, there goes another one! Do you think I'll *ever* get the hang of this?"

There was some high-pitched laughter, and I could hear my mother joining in.

It was such a pleasant sound.

But my surprises for the day weren't over yet.

Reaching the stable, I quickly found what I was looking for and started back toward the house.

Coming toward me, clutching a heavy iron bucket almost as big as he, was David, Agathe's son.

I rushed toward him. "David, what are you doing?"

"I'm fine, Miss Rebecca. Just taking out the ashes," he said.

"Here, let me help you!" I reached for the handle.

He stopped and moved the bucket out of my reach.

"It's more than my life is worth, Miss Rebecca," he said, "to let you get your pretty clothes all dirty."

I smiled and dropped my hand.

"Well, at least let me open the bin for you."

"Okay. You can do that."

I followed the independent little man around the side of the stable to the back alley.

There, I flipped the catch and swung the lid on the largest of the four barrels standing in regimental order against the fence. A familiar white board, leaning against the inside of the barrel caught my eye.

"Well, what's this?" I said, reaching for it.

"Oh, careful, miss!" David said. "I'm sure it's very dirty!"

He lifted his bucket and tipped its contents into the bin.

I jumped back as an ashy cloud billowed out.

"Well, what is it?" I asked again.

"It's the measurer from your front gate," David said, setting down his bucket and fastening the lid back on the bin.

"The measurer? But who . . . ?" An image of Kris suddenly flashed through my mind.

"It was your father," David said. "He took a hammer out there last night and pulled the whole thing right off. Then he got a saw and cut the two tall posts on your gate down to just above the gate itself."

"So another board could never be put up," I said softly.

"Pardon me, miss?"

"Nothing, David. Just thinking."

David smiled. "Well, I'd better get back," he said. "Mama is cleaning out the fireplaces to get ready for winter."

"Of course she is," I said. "She takes very good care of us."

David smiled and scurried off toward the house.

Another big change in my life happened just before Christmas.

Kris asked to meet with Papa.

I had no idea what it was about, but when Papa told me they were meeting, for some unaccountable reason, my heart began to race.

I greeted Kris just inside the door and took his hat and coat.

"What are you talking to my father about, Kris?"

He leaned forward, his eyes twinkling and said, "Shh! It's a great secret!"

I scowled at him.

"Careful, Becs." He grinned, touching my chin with a gentle finger. "Your face will freeze that way."

I laughed and batted his hand away.

He nodded. "That's my girl," he said.

"Ah, Kris," Papa said. "I thought I heard you rattle."

Kris chuckled.

I turned.

Papa was standing in the doorway of his study.

"Well, come in, son, come in."

Papa put his arm around Kris's broad shoulders and pulled him inside.

Mama came around the corner from the kitchen, a stack of neatly-folded towels in her arms. "Who was that?"

"Oh, it was just Kris," I said.

"Oh, right. The meeting with Papa." Mama peered at me suddenly. "Any idea what it's about?"

"None whatever," I said.

Mama smiled. "Well, I guess we'll know soon enough."

She was right.

A short time later, Papa asked Mama and I to join he and Kris in the parlor.

"I'm not sure of the correct procedure in matters like these," Papa said after we were seated. "So I guess I'll just announce it." He smiled at me, then looked at Kris, fidgeting uncharacteristically in front of the fireplace.

"Kris has asked to formally pay court to Rebecca."

Mama clapped her hands together. "Oh, how nice," she said.

It took a moment, though, for his words to make sense to me.

Then I felt my mouth widen in a big smile. Now my racing heart could be explained. It had known what I had not.

"If you'll have me," Kris said softly, walking over to my chair and making a deep bow.

I stood up and offered him both of my hands. "Of course I will!" I said.

He squeezed my hands and gave me a quick kiss on the cheek.

CHAPTER SIX

*O*ur little community accepted the change in Kris's and my relationship with an outward show of support and acceptance.

But sometimes I wondered what their real feelings were.

"So you're courting the Diene-lover, are you?" Bert said to me as we were standing in line for food at the harvest festival.

"Please don't call Kris that," I said softly. "I mean, he does love the Elves, but he loves everyone." I looked pointedly at Bert. "Including fools and children." I smiled.

Bert made a face.

"And face it, Bert, it's nothing more than the rest of us should do."

He snorted loudly and several people standing near turned to look at us.

"Bert! Keep your voice down!" I said.

"Why? Don't want everyone to know that good old Kris is a Diene-lover?"

I frowned at him. "Of course that's not what I meant."

"Then what?"

"I just don't want anyone else to hear us, that's all." I glanced over at the long tables of food and at the Elves who were serving.

"Ah. I see. You just don't want your new friends to hear us," Bert said. He snorted again. "Like it matters! They don't have feelings anyway. At least, not like we do."

"I'm afraid you're mistaken, Bert, old friend," Kris spoke up from behind us.

We both spun around.

"Kris! Didn't see you, old man," Bert said, coloring slightly.

"So I guessed," Kris said, grinning.

He looked at me. "Had anything to eat yet, dear?"

I looked down at the clean plate I was holding, then at the line up of people in front of me and grinned.

"What does the evidence say?"

"It says that my girl is starving," Kris said, laughing. "Here. Let me take your place, and you go and find a spot for us to sit down."

"Oh, no. I'd rather stay here with you," I said.

"Well, I don't know. Aren't there rules against people cutting into line?"

"Yes!" a loud voice said from further back in the line.

Everyone laughed.

"Seriously, Kris, stand up with your girl," the person behind us said. "We really don't mind!"

"Speak for yourself!" the same voice back in the line said.

Again, everyone laughed.

"I promise I won't take all of the food," Kris said, trying to bat his eyes coaxingly.

"Give it up, Kris," I said, smiling. "It only works for Margaret."

"I know." Kris sighed.

"Here, Master Kris," a high voice said. "You should have something to put your food on."

We looked down. Agathe was standing in front of us, holding out a clean plate.

"You're so right, Agathe," Kris said. "How thoughtful of you!"

Agathe giggled. "And we have a nice spot for you two to sit when you're ready," she said. Then she quickly rejoined the other Elves behind the large table.

Everyone around us went quiet, watching the little Elfa.

"Teacher's pet," Bert said, breaking the silence.

We were directed to a comfortable spot beneath one of the large trees on the boulevard.

"Becs, I've been thinking," Kris said.

"Oh, dear," I said.

He grinned and stuck a large piece of turkey into his mouth.

Chewing thoughtfully, he looked up at the cloudless, blue sky.

"Sure is a beautiful day for the middle of November," he said.

"Yes. I can't believe we're actually able to sit outdoors for the harvest supper this year. I've never known it to happen before."

He was silent for a moment, chewing.

"What were you thinking about, Kris?" I said, finally.

He looked at me, swallowed carefully, and took a breath. "Well, about the children," he said.

I looked around the park. Dozens of families sitting together eating and laughing.

"What about the children?"

"Oh, not these children, Becs. These are fine. Well-fed, happy."

"Well, what children, then?"

"The children who *aren't* well fed and happy."

"Kris, you're such a tease! What children?"

He sobered. "Becs, most of the children who don't live in our part of town go to bed hungry nearly every night."

"What?"

"It's true. I have been trying to think of ways to help them."

"Kris, you mean to tell me that there are children in our city who don't have enough to eat?"

"Ah, Becs, I can't blame you for not knowing. We are all the product of our situation."

"What?"

He sighed. "Yes, Becs, there are many, many children who lack even the necessities of life."

I was silent. I couldn't imagine one child in want, let alone dozens.

"I feel that there must be something we can do to help them."

"And you must let us help," a squeaky little voice spoke up.

We both turned.

Hank was standing behind us, with a tall pitcher in one hand. "I'm here to refill your glasses, if you would like," he said.

I shook my head and smiled, but Kris held out his nearly empty glass.

"Thanks, Hank," he said.

"It's my pleasure," Hank said.

"Now what was it you were saying?" he asked the Elf.

"I heard what you were saying to Miss Rebecca," Hank said. "And the Elves would like to help."

Kris stared at him. "Really?"

"Close your mouth, Kris. You look silly," I whispered.

He snapped his lips shut. "Really?" he said again.

Hank laughed. "Really," he said. "If there are children suffering, we would like to help."

"But you . . . but you . . . but . . ." Kris was at a loss for words. He tried again. "You don't have . . ."

"Master Kris, only one thing matters. That there are children suffering, and we are in a position to help."

"Well now, I've experienced everything," Kris said softly.

"I highly doubt that," Hank said, grinning, "but we'll see what we can do."

❄ ❄ ❄

After several closed-door meetings with Papa, Kris and a large group of Elves set up a workshop in the unused half of our barn.

Then followed noisy hammering and sawing and the general sounds of abused wood.

Not wanting to intrude, I stayed away for as long as I could—one month.

During that time, to keep my mind from the activities in the stable, Mama introduced me to the new and wondrous activities accorded to women who had officially achieved "adulthood."

Morning calls.

I had never been so bored.

The giving and receiving of bits of pasteboard. The strict rules of decorum. The "chatting." Saying one thing while your eyes said another. Everything about it made no sense.

Fortunately, the snow arrived. A lot of it. And with the snow, there came a reluctance to step outside in fancy leather boots.

Reprieve.

I pulled on my ratty old fur boots and a worn wool coat, and I wandered out to have a long-delayed peek.

Kris met me as I entered.

"Oh, Becs, I was hoping you'd come," he said. He steered me through throngs of Elves, each busily and attentively working on some project.

I could recognize partially finished bits of furniture and what looked like several different carvings of animals.

Kris guided me to one of the larger back rooms and slid the door open.

I stopped in the doorway, amazed.

The room that had once held mounds of fresh hay now housed child-sized tables, chairs, benches, beds, and other furniture. Every imaginable wooden toy filled the place: Wagons and coaches. Animals. Farm buildings and fences. Dolls. Doll carriages. Tiny doll furniture and stately doll homes. Carousels.

Everything that any child could possibly wish for, all cunningly and beautifully made.

"Kris, this is . . . wonderful!" I said. "Well, 'wonderful' hardly seems adequate, but I can't think of anything that expresses it better."

Kris took my hand and pressed it. "*Wonderful* suits me fine," he said. "You really like them?" He picked up a tiny chair and held it out.

I leaned forward and peered closely at the finely turned spindles forming the legs.

I shook my head. "I don't think I've seen finer work," I said.

"Nor I," Kris said, setting the chair down once more.

"And that's not all." He pulled me back into the main room, then moved to another door.

This room had held grain and supplements for the horses.

"Just look at what's in here."

Again, he slid the door back. The grain, indeed any

trace of it, was gone. Now the room was piled high with . . . heaps of cloth.

I moved closer.

Clothing. Frocks and skirts. Hats, shirts, trousers, and coats. Small leather shoes and boots.

"Excuse me," a little voice said.

I turned to allow an Elfa to move past me. She set another pair of leather boots on the growing pile, smiled at the two of us, and turned to go.

"Thank you, Erna," Kris said.

Her dark eyes sparkled as she nodded and skipped from the room.

"Kris, this is amazing!" I said, lifting a coat from the top of a stack. "Look at this! The workmanship is amazing! Look at the tiny stitches!"

"I have," he said. He moved further into the little room and spread his arms wide. "I can't believe what those Elves turn out. Nor the speed at which they do it."

He smiled. "It's almost magical," he added. "I leave in the evening, and when I come back in the morning, they have managed to make a dozen more items. And each better than the last!"

I smiled. "Well, there *are* a lot of them," I said, walking back to the door and glancing into the main room. I smiled at the Elves boiling everywhere.

He shook his head. "It's more than that, Becs," he

said. "If you had a hundred humans here, they still couldn't do what these Elves are doing."

"Well, they're talented, then."

"Oh, I'll give you that." Kris grinned.

I set the coat carefully on the stack and gave it a pat.

It was such beautiful clothing. Then I remembered what Kris had said. "But, Kris, you said the children were starving. How are these toys and things going to feed them?"

"Well, many of them are underfed, Becs," he said. "But they are also underdressed as we head into the coldest months of the year."

"Okay, that explains the clothing, coats, and shoes."

He grinned. "You don't give up, do you?"

"No."

"Well, a lot of the toys and children's furniture will go to the needy children. But a lot more will be sold to the wealthy families."

"Ah, I see. And the money will be used to buy the needed food."

"There's nothing slow about you, Becs." Kris grinned.

"That's what makes me so nice," I said.

He laughed. "Our only problem has been that the wealthy families don't want furniture made by Elves."

"Stupid," I said.

"You stole the words from my tongue."

"So what are you doing about it?"

"Well, your papa has been a great help in that area," he said.

"My papa?"

"He actually gave us the money and tools to start this enterprise," Kris said.

"And the materials?"

"Oh, those come mostly from the Elves."

"Ah. From the woods."

"Exactly. I guess they have access to quite a stock of seasoned lumber," Kris said.

I thought of the furniture in the other room. "I guess they do."

"Anyway, your papa has also been our salesman."

"Papa?"

He nodded. "He has started a company that specializes in children's toys and furniture. As far as his customers know, everything is made by his 'company.' They don't care who actually operates the tools as long as they are operating under the umbrella of some human."

"It all seems so ridiculous," I said.

"It truly is," Kris said. "But it is working. Already, our sales are mounting, and the quality and workmanship are being touted into other counties. Even other countries."

"And that's what counts."

He smiled. "We have been able to start deliveries of food and other necessities to the poorer families."

"Oh, I'm so glad," I said.

"I'd like to have you come with me sometime," he said.

"I'd love to."

CHAPTER SEVEN

The sleighs were stacked high with furniture, toys, food, and clothing.

The Elves piled into the back one, worming their way into every available space.

"Where's a spot for me?" I asked, standing in the snow beside the lead sleigh.

"You're not so very big," Kris said, laughing. "Here." He patted the seat. "You can sit beside me."

I raised my eyebrows and regarded the tiny spot. "Both of us? There?"

"It'll be cozy."

"Is *that* what you call it!"

He laughed again.

"Come on, Becs," he said. "Let's get going before the horses freeze."

I sighed and let him swing me aboard and hand me a lap robe. Then I settled into the soft leather seat and tried to give him as much room as I could.

He climbed up after me and draped the wonderfully warm fur over both of us.

He was right. This was cozy.

I breathed a huge cloud of white vapor into the air. This was fun!

Kris unhooked the reins and held them up. "Okay, boys, let's show Rebecca what we can do!"

A snort from the lead horse and we were off.

It was exhilarating—the cold breeze in our faces, the warm fur above and the hot bricks below keeping us from getting chilled.

All too soon, he was whistling to the team and they were pulling over to the side of the road.

"First stop, Becs," Kris said, climbing down.

"But we just got started," I protested.

"Hard to believe that the needy live so close to you?"

"Well, yes. I mean, no. I mean . . . I was just enjoying the ride."

"Me, too, Becs," Kris said, smiling at me warmly. "But this is our first stop."

I turned and looked at the tiny home perched almost on the sidewalk.

It leaned a little toward the right and the two front windows had both been replaced by crookedly nailed, mismatched boards.

As we crossed the walk, the door opened slightly.

"Yes?" a woman's voice asked. "What is it you want?"

"We don't want anything, Mrs. Baer," Kris said. "We're here to help."

The door inched open a tiny bit more.

"Help?"

"We have food and supplies for the children."

The door opened still further. We could now see a slender woman, with a worn face and bright blue eyes.

She was dressed in what looked like every scrap of clothing she owned. And I do mean "scrap."

"Supplies for the children?"

"May we come in, Mrs. Baer?"

The door opened and she stepped back. "Please," she said.

The two of us stepped into a tiny, bare entryway.

Mrs. Baer closed the door carefully and wrapped her patched and worn shawl more tightly around her shoulders.

I couldn't help but notice the plume of my breath. There. Inside the house.

Somehow it wasn't as romantic or exhilarating any more.

I glanced around. The one room of the house was painfully clean. There was no clutter. No clothes hanging on the bare hooks.

Nothing, in fact, that would suggest that someone

lived here until we saw the four children, ranging in age from about three to eight, covered in a collection of ragged, threadbare quilts and sitting up in a small, iron bed, pushed against the far wall.

There was no other furniture. No other "belongings."

Shelves on the wall opposite the bed contained a few cracked and mismatched dishes and a pot or two, but little food, further evidence of the family's poverty.

A fireplace, cold now and swept clean, covered most of one wall. A pitifully small bucket of partially burned wood stood to one side. A length of stovepipe sticking forlornly through the wall was ineffectively closed off with a wad of rags.

"You have no heat, Mrs. Baer?" I asked.

She glanced up at me shyly.

"No," she said briefly. "I had to sell our stove for food."

"But the fireplace."

She glanced at it. "Well, it costs money for the wood or coal," she said. "So we just light it for cooking."

I caught my bottom lip between my teeth and bit down hard. Tears wouldn't help at this moment, I was sure.

"Well, we're here to make things right," Kris said, giving his chuckle.

Instantly, the youngest child scrambled out from

under the covers. "Are you an angel?" he asked.

Again that chuckle. "No, son, I'm definitely not an angel," he said. "But I am here to help."

"I knew it," the little boy said.

"Amos, get back into bed," his mother said. "You'll get chilled out here."

"I'm tired of being in the bed," the little boy said. "I want to move around."

"Well, all right. But only for a few minutes. If you get cold, you have to crawl back in."

"Okay."

"So we have a few things for your family," Kris said. "Do you mind if we bring them in?"

Mrs. Baer studied Kris's handsome face for a moment.

His cheeks were red from the cold. He was wearing a red stocking cap and his blond hair had been whipped back by the chill wind because he had driven the sleigh.

But it was his smile that dominated. That smile was contagious.

Suddenly her lips parted in an answering smile. "No. No, I don't mind," she said softly. "I'd be grateful."

"Good," Kris said. He glanced over at the bed. "Why don't you cuddle under the blankets with your kids and stay warm. We'll try to be as quick as we can."

Mrs. Baer moved over to the bed and slipped under

the covers. Then, four pairs of eyes watched us.

"So what are you going to do?" the little boy asked, standing with sturdy, stockinged feet braced apart and red hands clasped behind him.

He looked up at Kris.

"Well, first of all, I'm going to call my friends," Kris said. "Then we have some work to do, so I need you to climb into the bed with your family."

The little boy frowned but did as he was told.

"Kris, where do you want me?" I said.

"Becs, I think the safest place for you is against the wall beside the bed."

"Safest?"

He laughed. "Well, you know our friends. When they get going, it's best to just stay out of the way."

"Oh." I backed up against the chill wall beside Mrs. Baer. "Okay."

Kris opened the door, and the house was instantly filled with Elves.

Several elves carried in a small, shiny new stove.

"Oh, my," Mrs. Baer whispered when they appeared. "A stove." She spent the rest of the time alternately exclaiming and sobbing quietly into the rags that covered her.

While some Elves hooked the new stove to the pipe, others unrolled a warm carpet, carried furniture, stocked shelves, lit fires, and replaced windows.

In a remarkably short amount of time, the tiny home was warm. Sturdy chairs stood before a crackling fire. A table was pushed to the wall beneath now-fully-stocked shelves.

Two new beds had appeared and all three were now shoved together against the wall and covered with thick, brightly colored blankets and quilts.

Sunlight streamed through two new windows and formed warm, multicolored pools of light on the new rug.

The family cautiously began to emerge from their blankets. They exclaimed over the thick rag rug that now covered the cold, warped floorboards.

They moved over to the fireplace and crowded around it, holding chilled hands to the heat.

A couple of the children moved to the window and peered through the new glass.

Then Kris began to bring in the new clothing.

By this point, all Mrs. Baer could do was cry.

I helped her to one of the chairs in front of the fire and pushed her down into it. Then I handed her one of the old, ragged quilts and let her use it to blot tears and blow her nose.

Kris and I matched sizes to children and soon all were warmly dressed and shod.

"Lunch is ready!" one of the Elves sang out.

"Perfect timing," Kris said. He knelt beside Mrs. Baer's chair. "Mother," he said softly. "Everything is ready. Come now and eat with your children."

Mrs. Baer lifted reddened eyes. "How can I ever thank you?" she asked.

Kris smiled. "Just take good care of these fine children," he said. "Keep this place warm. We'll make sure that there is plenty of coal or wood so you don't have to worry about letting the fire go out. And we'll make sure that there is food on your shelves too."

Mrs. Baer looked over at the new table, now set with sturdy new dishes and with a large pot of stew gently puffing out steam. She sniffed the air. "It smells wonderful," she said, slowly getting to her feet.

"Trust me, it is," Kris said. "The Elves are terrific cooks."

"Elves. I—I didn't know," she said.

"There are probably a lot of things about Elves you didn't know," Kris said, grinning. He waved a hand. "They made all of this, including your stove and your clothes."

"The Elves . . ." Mrs. Baer stared at them. "I didn't know," she said again.

"Well, spread the word," Kris said.

Mrs. Baer looked at him. "I will."

Kris stood up. "We've left some extra clothes for you and the children," he said, glancing toward the now-filled hooks.

Mrs. Baer blinked away a new flood of tears. "How can I ever thank you?" she asked again.

Kris grinned. "Like I said before, just look after these precious children. And if you see someone who needs help, help."

"Oh, I will," Mrs. Baer said. She called her children to her.

"Tell these nice people thank you," she said.

There was a chorus of timid "thank-yous."

"You're very welcome," Kris said.

"We'll leave you," I said. "Bless you!"

"Bless you!" she said.

We stepped out into the sunshine.

"You *are* an angel," a small voice said from the doorway. "Angels help."

Kris and I looked back at the small face framed in the partially opened door.

"I guess we are," he said, smiling.

The door shut.

I took a deep breath, then turned to Kris. "That was the single most wonderful experience of my life," I said.

He smiled. "Mine too."

We visited three more houses, slowly emptying the sleighs and delivering warmth and food and hope to other families.

Finally, happily tired, Kris started for home.

"Thank you, Kris," I said.

"For what?"

"For bringing me along to see what you do."

"I'm afraid that I am the one who benefited," he said, chuckling. "I got to look at you all day."

I shook my head and laughed. "You are easily pleased!"

He laughed with me.

"You know, when I first met you, I thought you were crazy," I said.

"Really. And what do you think now?"

"Oh, I still think you're crazy. But it's a crazy I like."

"Oh. Well. Good, I think," Kris said, laughing.

CHAPTER EIGHT

I went with Kris on many of his deliveries after that.

It was heart-warming.

And humbling.

On Christmas Eve, he made the biggest run of all. Four sleighs.

And this time, I wasn't allowed to go because they left after dark and didn't come back until dawn.

I was watching through the window for their return.

I heard the bells long before I saw their lanterns.

Then, a large sleigh slowed in front of the house.

As Kris skillfully directed the team into the drive and around to the back of the house, I hurried into coat and boots and made my way as quietly as possible to the service entrance.

I met Kris as he was handing the reins to Hank at the stable door.

"How did it go, Kris?" I said.

He spun around. "Oh, Becs, I'm sorry! Did I wake you?"

"I've not been to sleep yet," I said. "I've been watching for you."

"Oh, my dear, you didn't have to do that!"

He put his arms around me and squeezed me tight. "But I'm glad you did," he whispered into my ear. "It's so nice to come back and find you here waiting."

I giggled and stuck a finger into my ear. "Kris, that tickles!" I said, wiggling my finger.

He laughed and released me. Then he took one hand and squeezed it. "Oh, Becs, it was so wonderful," he said softly.

"Tell me about it!" I said eagerly.

"Let's go somewhere warm," he said. "And chaperoned."

I giggled again. "Well, everyone is in the house, but they wouldn't be much use to us," I said, "being asleep as they are."

Kris chuckled. "You're right. That would never do." He glanced at the stable door. "Let's go in here. There are plenty of Elves to see to the proprieties."

He pulled my hand through his arm and led me inside.

The front half of the stable was in deep shadow. A

couple of horses stuck their heads over the half-doors of their stalls and nickered softly. Kris patted their soft noses gently as we passed.

Finally we were in the workshop. Even though it was a few minutes before dawn, the place was bustling. Elves scurried everywhere, engaged in one task or another.

But there was little noise.

"What's going on?" I said. "Usually, it's deafening in here."

Kris smiled. "Well, it is Christmas day," he said. "And all of the tasks we set for ourselves have been completed."

"Then why are the Elves here?"

He glanced around, his eyes twinkling fondly. "Well, they are busily planning next year."

"Next year?"

"Yes. We're planning on making this Christmas Eve delivery an annual thing."

"Really?"

"Oh, Becs, it was so wonderful."

I sat down on a sawhorse and let my feet swing. "Tell me about it."

He straddled an anvil and sat down opposite me. "Well, you know that most of the families in need have been cared for."

"Yes, you and Papa were talking about that earlier this week."

"Well, he and I and the Elves decided that Christmas Eve would be a good time to give the children of the city things they really don't need to survive. Things they can play with. That will help them be children."

"Oh, what a wonderful idea!" I said, clapping my hands.

Kris grinned. "Well, I thought so," he said. "So we delivered toys and games and puzzles and books. Oh, stacks of items that would help them play. Relax. Enjoy a tiny little bit of childhood."

He leaned his head back. "I don't know what it was, but with every package and parcel we left, the feeling of happiness and goodwill seemed to deepen, grow stronger."

He looked at me once more, his blue eyes twinkling. "I'll never forget that feeling, Becs," he said. "I wanted it to go on and on and on."

"Watch out, or you will be delivering packages to children the world over!" I said, laughing.

He sobered at once. "The world over, you say."

I stared at him. "Oh, Kris, I was just teasing. No one could possibly take gifts to all of the children in the world! It would take months. Months and months!"

But he didn't hear me. His brow had furrowed and

he was obviously giving my suggestion more consideration than I thought it deserved.

Then he blinked and took a deep breath. He looked at me and grinned once more.

"So, Becs, you think our toy delivery is a good idea?"

"Oh, better than good, Kris," I said. "In fact, I think you're a genius!"

He laughed again.

Then he sobered once more. "Becs, how would you feel about being married to this genius?"

The words were spoken so quietly that, for a moment, I didn't realize what he had said.

"Pardon?" I said.

"Marry me, Mary Rebecca Hahn. Make me the happiest man in the world."

"Oh, but Papa . . ."

"I've already spoken to your father. He has given his blessing."

"He has? When?"

Kris smiled. "Oh, a long time ago," he said.

"Really? How long?"

"Well, when I first asked to court you," he said. "You know what an efficient person I am. I figured, 'why waste time with two conversations?'"

"But I . . ."

He put gentle, work-roughened fingers against my

lips. "Now no more talk," he said, "unless it's yes or no." He grinned at me. "Preferably yes."

I giggled and held out my arms. "It's yes, Kris, but did you have any doubt?"

The wedding was planned for June. Just before my seventeenth birthday.

"I had my doubts, dear," Mama was saying, while we were sitting beside a warm fire early in January. "Oh, yes. Serious doubts."

"But Mama . . ."

She shushed me with a wave of her hand. "Oh, I knew he was a fine man who would work hard all his life and would never harm you. But I was concerned about whether he could provide for you."

I thought of the countless families he had "provided for" and hid a tiny smile. "Really?"

"Well, he didn't seem to have a profession, did he? And his father, though his holdings were by all accounts large, was dead, and the family had been literally stripped of their possessions."

She laid her knitting on her lap and rubbed her eyes. "Oh, this light is getting bad for handwork. Perhaps I'll stop for the night."

"Go on, Mama," I said. "You were talking about Kris's family."

"Oh, yes. Where was I?" She wrinkled her smooth brow slightly. "Oh, yes. Well, he didn't have anything, really, and, let's face it, there are many in the neighborhood who think him rather strange."

"Well, it's their loss," I said hotly.

Mama patted my knee. "I know, dear, I know," she said. "But, taken as a whole picture, he didn't present himself as a young man worthy of my daughter." She put out a soft, white hand and grasped my chin gently, smiling at me tenderly.

I slipped to my knees beside her chair and wrapped both arms around her waist. "Well, I'm glad you changed your mind," I said.

"Well, it was you that did that," Mama said, patting my shoulder.

"Me? How?"

"When you talked to Papa and I about the Elves."

"Really?" I slid back onto my chair.

"Really," she said, smiling. "You pointed out things that I just hadn't thought of."

"Well, I'm glad," I said.

"As am I." She sighed. "But I still had grave misgivings about your intended husband."

"Why?"

"No profession," she said.

I was thoughtful for a moment. "So how is it different now?"

"Well, now he has this company."

"What company?"

"The one making all of the children's furniture."

"The company? But I thought . . . I thought . . ."

"We know what you thought. That Papa owned the company and that all of the furniture and toys were made by him." She shook her head. "Not true." Her eyes twinkled.

"Kris owns it?"

"Correct."

"Maybe he should have told me."

❄ ❄ ❄

"So if we're going to be partners in life, we need to be just that," I said, sitting down on the footstool. "Partners."

Kris's eyes were twinkling. "Is that really what you want, Becs?" he said.

"You know me, Kris. I don't like to be left out."

"Oh, I do know that," he said, chuckling.

He got to his feet. "Wait here," he said. He hurried from the room.

We had been sitting in front of the great fireplace in the Bauer home.

Abel had excused himself some time earlier and Kris's mother and aunt and uncle were nowhere to be seen.

I stayed where I was on the footstool. It was comfortable and within perfect toasting distance of the crackling flames.

Soon Kris was back. Carrying a large, wooden box.

"Here, Becs," he said, setting it on the carpet in front of me.

"What's this?" I said.

"This constitutes the greatest contribution you can make to our business," Kris said. "That is, unless you would rather swing an axe or use a planer or saw."

"Umm, no. Maybe I'd better see what's in here."

He laughed. "These, my dear, are the letters and correspondence that have come in to the company since our Christmas Eve toy delivery."

"Really?" I stared into the box, which I could now see held dozens of envelopes and papers.

"Really. They contain the gratitude and wishes of countless children."

I picked up one much-folded scrap of paper.

"Too the Angles Hoo Gav Us Crismus" was printed

in crude letters which sloped determinedly toward the upper right-hand corner.

I unfolded it.

"Thank you!" was all it said.

"Oh, Kris, this is sweet!"

He smiled. "There are many, many more, just like that one."

"So what is it you want me to do with them?"

"I want them filed. Neatly and efficiently so they can be found at a moment's notice. Then I want you to compile the information that is on them, for future use."

I had pulled out another while he was speaking. "Oh, Kris, listen to this one . . ."

> *Dear Angels,*
>
> *Thank you for your gifts. My little brother is resting comfortably now, thanks to you. He says his hip hardly hurts anymore. Mama says that Angels come when we are good, so I will try my best to be good and to work extra hard all year, so you will remember him next Christmas. This letter was written by . . .*

"Obviously someone who made use of a letter writer," Kris said softly.

"Oh, Kris, this is wonderful!" I said, folding it up

neatly once more. "So you want me to answer these letters?"

"Yes. And sort through them. And start making lists of needs and wishes."

"And boys and girls who are good?"

He laughed. "Definitely a list of the good. And bad, for that matter."

I dropped the second letter back into the crate. "Please bring the list to me when you come to dinner tonight," I said.

"I'll bring it now," he said, stooping and picking up the case. "That way you can get started right away."

"Slave driver!"

He chuckled.

CHAPTER NINE

For the next few months, I was kept busy, both with arrangements for our wedding and in dealing with the letters and cards that kept coming steadily in.

Each morning I would be awakened by a tap on my door, followed by Agathe, with the newly arrived messages. Some were no more than short notes of appreciation. Others were quite involved and truly heartrending.

I was appalled at the conditions under which some children were being raised.

I'm afraid I got quite vocal about it on occasion.

"What do you mean, Dr. Rempe, that children aren't deserving of assistance until they have earned it?"

"Well, I . . ." The expensively-dressed young man looked around for help.

All eyes in the theater lobby were on us.

I felt my lips curve into a gentle smile and I raised my eyebrows. "Well?"

"All I'm saying is that everyone should contribute to the wealth of a nation," he said.

"Have you ever seen a two-year-old child swing a hammer, Doctor?"

"Well, no, I . . ."

"They don't do it very well," I said. "Most of them can't even pick one up."

"Well, of course I was thinking of tasks much more suited . . ."

"What tasks do you think a two-year-old child could do, Doctor?"

"Well, I'm sure I don't know . . ."

"*Anything* as far as I'm concerned," I said, turning away. "Kris, take me out of here. I've heard enough. I'm no longer in the mood for theatrics."

Kris chuckled as he took my hand and slid it through the crook in his arm. "Well, you certainly gave that young man something to think about," he said.

"I'd like to give him something else entirely," I murmured.

Kris laughed. "That's my girl!"

"It just makes me so mad. Children working! It's the stupidest thing I've ever heard of."

"And yet it happens."

"It does," I said, sadly.

❋ ❋ ❋

"But do you realize that we have to still associate with these people, Rebecca?"

"I'm sorry, Mama, but he was just so . . . insufferable."

"Rolf, speak to her," Mama said, looking at my father, seated at the far end of the table.

Papa put down his fork and lifted a snowy napkin to his lips. He got to his feet and made a slight bow to Mama. "If you will excuse us, Mary, my dear?"

"Certainly, Rolf," Mama said, her lips curving into a smile.

Papa looked at me. "If you are quite finished, Becca?"

I sighed. "I guess I am," I said, rising also.

He stepped back and let me precede him to his study. I slipped into the room and perched on an over-sized chair near the fire.

Papa closed the door and took the chair next to mine. Then he sighed deeply.

"Better get it over with, Papa," I said.

He looked at me, and I was surprised to see the twinkle in his eyes.

"Papa, you're . . . are you happy?"

"So happy, my dear," he said, chuckling. "And so proud."

"Oh," I said in a small voice. "I thought you were angry."

"Of my daughter going to battle for those who can't fight for themselves? Never."

I relaxed. "Then why did you bring me here?"

He sobered, then got up and walked over to his desk.

"Papa?"

He shuffled a couple of papers, stacking them neatly.

Finally, he turned. "It was for quite another reason that I wanted to talk to you," he said. He cleared his throat. "I've been thinking about something for some time. Actually, I have been thinking about it for . . . some years. It has weighed more heavily recently."

"For goodness' sake, Papa! What is it?"

He looked at me. "There is something you should know, Rebecca," he said. "In fact, it's something both you and Kris should know before you marry. Something I should have told you long ago."

"What is it, Papa?"

He sighed. "It's not easy for me to say," he said. "It concerns a family secret."

"Secret?"

"Yes. Something that even your mother doesn't know, though I'm quite sure she suspects."

"Goodness gracious, Papa. Tell me."

He half smiled. "I guess there's nothing to do but

say it," he said. He came over and took my hands. "Your grandmother was an Elf, Rebecca," he said, softly.

It took a moment for the words to sink in.

I stared at him. "An Elf."

He nodded sadly. "I never wanted to keep it from you," he said. "And I certainly didn't want to keep it from your mother." He released my hands and walked over to the fireplace to poke at the glowing logs there. "But I just didn't have the . . . courage," he whispered. "I thought I'd lose her."

He rubbed a hand across his face, then came over and sat down once more. "I guess I'd better start at the beginning," he said.

"Always a smart move," I said.

He smiled, then took a deep breath and, leaning back in his chair, looked up toward the ceiling. "My father was an orphan. The last of his line," he said, finally. "He chose the profession of woodcarver and, in keeping with his line of work, lived far from here, in the forest. Actually very near an Elf village. His location and isolation put him in constant association with the Elves. He fell in love with the daughter of the High Elf. And married her."

He looked at me. "They were very much in love. Probably any human who knew about it would have had something to say, but the Elves, being the loving

beings they are, gave them nothing but support. They were happy."

He sighed. "But as in any good love story, there must be tears. My father's came much sooner than he expected. My mother died shortly after I was born." He looked down and laced his fingers together. "I guess having me was too much for her," he said.

"After her death, my father simply couldn't stay there any longer. He said there were too many memories. He packed me up and, with a couple of his closest Elf friends, came to live here."

He looked at me. "Like you, I too didn't show any signs of my Elf parentage. Though I had my mother's dark hair and eyes, I had my father's ears and stature."

He gripped my hand tightly. "I want you to know that my father was not ashamed of his love," he said. "For my sake, once he realized the attitude of the humans here toward Elves, he felt it prudent that our secret remain ours. He was simply a widower with one son. Wife, deceased. Heart, broken. That was what the world saw and no one ever questioned further. Or if they did, I didn't hear about it."

He sighed. "We went about our lives. He, making a new one. Me, being the spoiled only son of a doting father."

Papa looked at me. "When you were born—and you

must know that it was a miracle that you were—and you didn't show any of the obvious outward signs . . ."

"Ears."

"Yes, those. You are short for a human, though, and I have always been afraid that someone would figure it out."

"No wonder you were so happy the day I was able to pass my first measurer."

"Yes. And at a reasonable age. You can't imagine the mix of pleasure and guilt I felt every time you said or did something that showed your human side."

"I think I can, Papa," I said slowly.

He put a hand on my shoulder. "So what do you think, Becca?" he said.

"I'm not sure, Papa," I said. "I don't think I've quite taken it in."

"I'll give you some time."

He got up. "It is quite a burden I have placed upon your small shoulders, Mary Rebecca. But I think you can handle it."

I tried to smile. "I'll try, Papa."

He turned and left the room.

A short time later, there was a knock at the study door.

"Anyone home?" Kris asked, coming into the room. "Your papa said I'd find you here."

"I'm afraid I've some news to tell you, Kris."

"Well, here I am."

I looked up at this tall, gentle man. The man I had promised to marry. The man who had changed my life.

How would my news affect him?

He reached for my hand. "Has it to do with you being part Elf?"

I felt my mouth drop open.

He chuckled. "I knew it from the moment I saw you," he said.

"But . . . but . . . how?"

"Well, when you spend the amount of time with Elves that I do, you pick up a few things," he said.

I shook my head. "This makes no sense," I said.

He chuckled again. "Oh, it will, Becs," he said. "It will."

❄ ❄ ❄

Kris and I were married in the garden of my family home on the sixth of June in the year 1810. It was a brief and beautiful ceremony.

As Kris kissed me for the first time as my husband, I heard the joyous shouts and cheers of Elves and humans. Together.

Another first. Then, there was the party. I don't remember much of it.

Apart from . . . colors.

The beautiful plants, coaxed into a magnificent show by the skilled fingers of countless Elf gardeners. White linens. Shining plate and crystal. Green, green leaves and grass. Impossibly blue sky.

It was a perfect day. A day of beginnings. Before I knew it, it was time for us to leave.

There were tears—bittersweet.

And then I was waving to our families as they stood at the end of the driveway.

My parents' arms were about each other as they waved back.

I settled back in the carriage seat and smiled at Kris. Finally I belonged, completely and wholeheartedly, to the amazing man I had married.

❅ ❅ ❅

After far too short a honeymoon in Paris, Kris brought me back to our city and introduced me to our new home, which he had secretly purchased and, just as secretly, remodeled and furnished.

"Oh, Kris, it's lovely!"

"I so hoped you would like it."

"Well, I do. I have only one complaint."

"What's that?"

"You should have told me."

"Becs, one thing you're going to have to get used to is the fact that I love surprises," Kris said, grinning.

"Hmm. I think I already know that."

"And I love surprising you."

I narrowed my eyes. "So this is part of the package?"

"It is."

I threw my arms around his neck and kissed his cheek. "Well, I'll just have to work on it, then."

"I'll give you plenty of practice."

I'm amazed at how quickly I was able to get used to married life. Maybe it was because I had married such a kind and considerate man, who made it his prime responsibility to keep me content.

Whatever the reason, I was blissfully, completely happy.

The years went by so quickly.

Chapter Ten

"No, I really don't need to buy anything," I said. "I just felt like a stroll downtown. The colors in the square are so pretty at this time of year."

Kris glanced at the flaming maple trees and grinned. "But as long as we're here, why don't I find something to surprise you with?" he said.

"You and your surprises," I scoffed.

He laughed.

Suddenly, from down the street, we heard raised voices. Or more correctly, one raised voice.

"You little tramp! How dare you try to cheat me!"

Kris's head came up and he peered intently forward. "Come on, Becs," he said. "Something's wrong."

He pulled me along the street.

There, parked at the curb was a fine buggy, with a beautiful but rather thin horse in the traces.

The animal had obviously been working hard. Her neck was coated with white froth, as were her sides around the straps of her expensive leather harness.

An Elf, dressed neatly in patched and worn breeches and coat, was standing near the head of the horse, a spilled bucket of grain on the pavement at his feet.

"But, Master," he was saying, "May needed something to eat . . ."

His voice trailed off as the short, rather heavy man standing on the curb stepped into the street, ignoring the large crowd that was gathering around them.

"I'll tell you when to feed her!" the man roared. "You stupid Diene! You'll have me in the poor house! I decide how much she gets!"

"But, Master, she has been working hard . . ."

The Elf cringed as his master's cane appeared suddenly in the air over his head.

"I'll teach you to obey me!"

The heavyset man swung the cane.

The Elf put up one arm and screamed as the finely-carved, polished wood connected.

There was a sickening crunch, and the Elf collapsed to the ground, cradling an obviously broken arm.

The cane was raised again.

But before the man could bring it down for a second blow, it was snatched from his grip. He spun around, his face purple with anger and outrage.

Kris calmly regarded him, the man's cane held in one large hand.

The man made a snatch for it, but Kris moved it just out of reach.

"I think we need to have a chat . . ." Again, he moved the cane. ". . . about the treatment of a man's servants . . ." Another attempt. ". . . and the proper uses for a cane."

Finally realizing that he wasn't going to succeed, the heavyset man dropped his arms to his sides and straightened his coat with a huff. "I'll have you arrested, my man," he said, leaning toward Kris and breathing heavily, "for stealing my property."

"I have stolen nothing, as these people can attest," Kris said, "Mr. . . . ?"

"Klein," the man said shortly, glancing around.

"Well, Klein, your cane is here," Kris said, holding it up, "as you can see."

"And you have no right to interfere when a man is disciplining his servant," Klein went on.

"Disciplining," Kris said. "Is that what you call it?"

The man began to look a bit uncomfortable as the crowd around him remained silent.

"Well, a man must retain authority," he said.

He glanced around at the set faces, hoping for some support.

A couple of people frowned and nodded. He took courage from this.

"Otherwise these Dienes will steal everything you have!" he said, a bit more loudly.

This time, several people nodded agreement.

"These *Dienes,* as you call them, are rational beings," Kris said quietly, "with thoughts and feelings."

Klein snorted. "Feelings!" he scoffed. "They can no more feel than . . . than . . ." He glanced at his horse. "Than my horse can feel."

Kris took a deep breath.

"You think this?" he said softly.

"I know this," Klein said smugly. "They don't feel things as we do. They simply can't. Why only last week . . ."

Faster than a wink, Kris whipped around and struck at Klein with his own cane, laying open one cheek.

I gasped audibly, as did many others in the crowd.

What the man had been going to say was forgotten as he screamed and clutched his face with both hands.

Kris leaned toward him. "They feel, Klein," he said. "And you'd better hope you never have to suffer like you make them suffer."

There was a sudden scuffle in the crowd as several men charged off up the street.

Kris threw the cane down on the stones and walked over to the Elf, still lying under the horse's front feet.

"Come, lad," Kris said. "Let's get you some help."

With Kris's aid, the Elf struggled to his feet, still clutching his injured arm.

"I thank you, Master . . ." he began.

"What's going on here!" a loud voice demanded.

I turned as an officer began to push his way through the crowd.

"This man assaulted me!" Klein screeched. "He stole my cane and beat me with it!"

The officer finally cleared the crowd. "What's that?"

Klein lowered his hands and showed the officer the bleeding gash on his round cheek. Then he pointed a bloodstained finger at Kris. "That man there!"

The policeman looked at the gash and frowned. Then he turned to Kris. "You do that?" he asked.

"I did," Kris said calmly.

"Any reason why?"

"The man had just used the cane to hit his servant," Kris said. "I didn't agree with his actions and thought he needed to be taught a lesson."

"His servant?"

Kris moved slightly aside, allowing the man a glimpse of the small, frightened Elf behind him.

"But it's a Diene," the officer said.

"He was abusing him," Kris said. "He broke his arm."

The officer stared at Kris. "So?"

"I want this man arrested!" Klein said. "I'm pressing charges!"

"Come along, sir," the officer said to Kris. "I'm afraid it's the lockup for you."

Kris shook his head. "I do protest, officer," he said.

"Protest all you want, sir, but the law is the law. You steal someone's property and assault someone and you are in violation."

"But what about Klein?" Kris demanded.

"Klein?"

"I'm Klein," the heavyset man said. "The one he assaulted."

"Klein assaulted his servant," Kris said, again indicating the Elf, now cowering close to the horse.

"He was disciplining his servant, sir," the officer said. "Nothing to do with me."

"Or the law," Kris said sadly.

"Come along, sir."

Kris shook his head again. Then he swung around. "You people, do you think this is fair?" he demanded. He nodded toward the Elf. "This Elf was intentionally injured for a rather minor mistake." Kris smiled slightly. "Actually, looking at this poor, underfed horse, I don't think it was a mistake. It was compassion."

Murmurs in the crowd.

"But for this action, he was thoroughly and horribly

'disciplined,'" Kris said. He looked around the crowd, then pointed at Klein. "And his master walks free."

Silence for several seconds.

"Well, he was a Diene," someone said.

Murmurs of agreement as the people started to drift away.

"You don't think they have feelings?" Kris went on. "That they should have rights?"

But he was speaking to an empty street.

Only Klein, the Elf, the officer, and I remained.

Kris slumped against the buggy.

"Come along, sir," the officer said. "Don't give me any trouble and I won't put you in irons."

He looked at Klein. "You'd better come too, sir," he said. "To swear out the warrant."

Klein nodded. He glanced at the Elf. "Diene!" he spat. "Take care of May!" He glanced at the bucket of spilled feed. "And see that you pick up every grain of that feed!"

Kris's eyes narrowed. He moved beside me. "Take care of the Elf, Becs," he said. "Make sure he gets the help he needs."

"I will, Kris."

"Come, sir."

"I love you, Becs," Kris said sadly, putting his arms around me.

I was surprised to feel his big body tremble.

"Kris, you're shaking!"

"I'm fine, Becs," he said. "Just the aftermath of yet another red-letter day for the Kringles."

"I'll come as soon as I can," I said.

"Wait a while," he said. "You know it takes a couple of hours to process me and get me into a cell."

I sighed. "I know."

He let me go, then touched my cheek with a calloused, gentle finger and turned to follow the officer up the street.

I watched them go. The officer, the accuser, and my Kris.

For a moment, the scene blurred.

Wiping my eyes, I took a deep breath and turned to the Elf.

He was under the horse's front feet, trying to pick up grains with his good hand while he cradled his broken arm between his waist and his legs.

"Here, lad, let me help," I said.

He glanced up at me. "Oh, mistress, no!" he said.

I narrowed my eyes at him. "Now, you . . . just what is your name?"

"Umm . . . Job, mistress."

"Well, Job, you sit there and rest," I said, firmly, seating him on the curb. "I will look after this mess."

He did as he was told and watched me as I scraped

the grain together and finally got it into the bucket.

"There," I said, nodding in satisfaction.

I looked up into the dark eyes of the patient horse and reached into the bucket. "And a handful for May. Just because."

Her soft lips picked delicately at the treat.

The Elf smiled.

"You're a kind one, mistress," he said softly.

"Almost as kind as the man that was just arrested," I said.

"I know who he is," the Elf said. "All of the People know who he is."

I smiled at him and stowed the bucket of grain in the back of the buggy. Then I pulled off my sash and wound it carefully around his arm and up around his neck, trying to give him a little support.

He looked at me. "It *was* Kris, wasn't it, mistress?"

I nodded and again dabbed at welling tears. "It was," I said, finally.

"I knew it when he snatched that cane," the Elf said quietly. "Saint Kris, or Santa Kris in the People's tongue, will always come to our aid."

Saint Kris? I closed my eyes and took a deep breath. "He always will," I said.

It took a while to find some help for Job.

No regular medical facility would take him.

Finally, I brought him back to our house to let Agathe care for him.

As we walked, he told me quite a bit about himself.

Job was the single father of two young children. The "smartest littles ever born," according to their doting dad.

His wife had died a couple of years after the youngest was born, in a nasty accident involving a carriage.

"I think of her often, mistress," Job said. "Especially late at night, when my littles are in bed."

"I'm so sorry for your loss, Job," I told him. "It must be especially hard, with your having to work and everything."

"Oh, it's not so bad," he said. "In the Elf community, all children are looked after, regardless of who is their actual parent. When I am at work, my two are as well fed and tended as they were when their dear mother was alive."

Another example of Elf superiority, I thought. But then I knew the depth of love and care they felt for everyone, children especially.

Job looked up at me. "Did you know, mistress, that Elves are coming from other places to live here in our city?"

"I didn't," I said. "Why?"

"Because of your husband," he said quietly.

I stopped and looked at him. "Because of Kris?"

He too stopped. "Yes, mistress. They know that wherever Kris lives, they will be safe."

"Oh," I said. It was all I could manage. I sighed. Well, Kris was obviously having *some* success. Unfortunately, it was the kind that only compounded his woes. Although he would never see it like that.

I sighed again.

"Are you all right, mistress?" Job asked.

"I'm fine, Job," I said, summoning up a smile.

I decided it was safer for me if we changed the subject. "Job, how long have your worked for Klein?"

"Oh, several years now," Job said, wrinkling up his brow in thought. "In fact, I had just started when my wife had her accident."

"Job," I said, suddenly suspicious. "Was it one of Klein's carriages?"

"It was, mistress," Job said softly. "The big one. He couldn't stop."

"She was run over by his carriage?"

"Yes, mistress. He likes to drive fast. It takes a while to get the horses stopped."

I stared at him, horrified. "Oh, Job, I'm so sorry!"

He patted my arm with his good hand. "It's all right, mistress. She's fine and happy, now."

I stared at him. "She is?"

"Oh, yes, mistress. She's with her mama now. Fine and happy."

Such faith. For a moment, I thought about Kris's gentle mother. She had passed quietly away not long after Kris and I were married. I wished that I could feel Job's conviction that she was "safe and happy," maybe even reunited with the husband she had loved so dearly.

I shook my head. "And you remained with Klein even after . . ."

"He is my master, mistress. Of course I would stay with him."

"But he was responsible . . ." I couldn't go on.

Job looked at me. "It was an accident, mistress. A terrible accident. He did not mean for it to happen."

"But . . . but . . ."

"Mistress, where would our world be if everyone filled their hearts with hate?"

I frowned and scratched my head. *About where it is*, I thought. "You're a better man than any of the *men* I've ever met, Job."

"Oh, no, mistress!" He grinned. "Just an Elf."

When we got Agathe cooed and harrumphed over his broken arm. "Well, I know exactly where to take you," she said. She looked at me. "With your permission, mistress?" she said.

"You don't need to ask my permission, Agathe," I said, smiling. "Just do what needs to be done."

She grabbed Job by his good arm and urged him toward the door.

"Thank you, mistress," he said as the two of them disappeared. "Thank you for everything!"

I followed them to the door. "Job! I want you to come back here after your arm is set," I called. "Promise me!"

"I will!" his voice came faintly across the yard.

I smiled. I hoped that I had found one more happy helper in my husband's company of workers.

Then I thought about Job and frowned. It might take some convincing.

❄ ❄ ❄

I pushed open the door of the jailhouse.

Several officers were standing about the room, talking and laughing together.

"Ah, Mrs. Kringle," the desk sergeant said. "Come in, dear, come in."

I sighed and approached the desk.

"They've just gotten him nicely settled," the man said. "Back in his usual cell."

"We've almost decided to put a sign over the door and reserve it just for your husband!" one of the men said.

The rest laughed.

I didn't join in.

"Just a moment," the desk sergeant said. "I'll take you to him."

The man reached up and unhooked a set of keys from a bank on the wall behind him.

"If you would please follow me," he said, politely.

He unlocked a door to the side of the desk and ushered me through.

I had walked down this long, gray hallway before. Countless times before. But tonight, it seemed more . . . dreary, somehow. The rough, gray stone seemed dull. Lifeless. Like I was feeling.

A lantern hung at the far end, where the cells were.

"Go ahead, Mrs. Kringle," the man said.

"Thank you, officer," I said.

I sighed and started down the hall. Soon, I was standing in a pool of light. A hand reached out of the cell on the far right.

"Becs, thank the Father you are here," Kris said.

I walked over and grasped his hand. It felt cold. Thin.

For the first time, I noticed that the veins showed plainly through the skin. My husband, who had always seemed so young and vibrant, was getting older.

As was I.

"I'll just leave the two of you alone," the sergeant

said. He set down a chair beside me and disappeared back up the hall.

"Oh, Kris," I said, putting my husband's hand to my face.

"I'm so sorry, my love," he said. "I'm sorry that I keep . . . causing trouble."

"Oh don't, Kris!" I said. "Don't start apologizing!"

"But I have to," Kris said.

"No. You don't!"

He gripped my hand tighter. "Becs, I don't think I'd survive without you," he said. "I'm sorry that the things I do keep putting me back in here." He glanced around his cell.

I followed his gaze.

Two plain, block walls. Bars between this and the next cell. A small cot with a thin, lumpy, bare mattress. A wool blanket. No window.

I looked back at the man I loved. He looked . . . tired. And there were bars separating us. Again.

"Oh, Kris," I sighed, thinking of the many, many times we had occupied these same positions after one of his numerous arrests.

He let go of my hand and, slumping down on the bed, put his head into his hands.

I sat on the chair and watched my husband.

"I'm so grateful that you stay with me, Becs," he

said. "Though I can't for the life of me figure out why."

"Can you not?" I said sharply.

He looked up.

"Kris, I believe in the things you do just as much as you do," I said. "I support your efforts completely!"

"Ah, Becs. You're one in a million," he said, grinning. "And I knew it the moment you became my partner in crime."

I made a face at him. "Okay, here's the thing," I said, "I really wasn't your partner in crime. I was just as shocked as the rest of the people."

He laughed. "I know. I'll never forget the look on your face when I pulled off the measurer."

"I must have looked pretty . . ."

"My mama had a word for it," Kris said. "Flabbergasted."

"Flabber . . . what?"

"Flabbergasted."

"You made that up."

"I really didn't. Maybe my mama did, but I didn't."

I rolled my eyes. "To get back to the point . . . I still remember the sound the measurer made when you wrenched it off the pole."

"Mrs. Schmidt was rather upset."

"And when you broke it over your knee. So calm." I shook my head. "I simply couldn't believe it."

"I couldn't believe that people could so blatantly display their prejudice for all to see," Kris said.

I was quiet for a moment. "You're right," I said. "I never thought of it quite that way before."

"It was like hanging a sign at the front gate that says, 'Look at us. We discriminate.'" He snorted softly.

"I know the reasons for everything you have done and do," I said. "And I understand why you do it . . ."

"Becs, you've seen them," Kris said quietly.

"What?"

"You've seen them. The Elves." He ran a hand through his graying blond hair. "You've seen them with their children. With their friends and spouses. With their fellow Elves."

"Yes," I said.

"They love each other. Truly love each other."

I nodded.

"And you've seen them with the humans. Being beaten and abused and humiliated. Being literally worked to death."

"I have," I said slowly.

"And in all of that, in everything they have been forced to submit to, they are kind, polite, and considerate. And they truly forgive and love their masters." He sighed. "They have a depth of love that we humans can only approximate." He paused. "Oh, we love. I don't

mean to say that we don't. But we love reservedly. They love completely. Without judgement and without holding back. A child's love. Without guilt. Or reservation. Or fear." He leaned back. "A perfect love."

He looked at me. "That is how I want to love, Becs," he said softly. "I want to love perfectly. As the Father loves . . ." He made a face. ". . . even the Kleins of the world."

"Oh, I don't know if I can love the Kleins of the world," I said.

"But don't you see, my dear? If we can't love men of Klein's ilk, how can we ever say that we love as the Elves do? Perfectly."

He sighed. "We must keep on trying," he said. "There is a power in that love, Becs. True, pure, righteous power."

"Then to gain it, perhaps we need to leave out the violence," I told him.

"You are right, my dear. That simply isn't me." He scowled. "I don't know what came over me."

"Well, the circumstances were dire," I said. "But I agree. Violence isn't you. No, if we're going to be like the Elves, we've got to be *like* the Elves. Patient under torment. Kind. Giving."

"You're right," Kris said, getting to his feet. "Becs, you're exactly right! Love thine enemy. Do good to

those who would hurt you or abuse you."

"Something like that," I said, smiling at him.

"Well, I've never been one for violence—" Kris said.

"Until today," I put in.

"Yes, well, let's put this day behind us and get back to work!"

"I couldn't agree more." He reached through the bars once more.

I stood up and he gripped my hands.

"Becs, we will somehow show the world how gentle and loving the Elves are. We'll show the humans how wrong they have been all these years."

"And we will do it by being *like* the Elves!"

The months and years and decades went by.

I kept my records. Kris ran the business of helping people—or Elves—in need. He delivered his Christmas toys. And loved everyone.

We never had any children of our own and, occasionally, I would find the time to wonder at our apparent inability to conceive, but as our home was filled with other people's children whom, in the Elf way, we were raising as our own, I was simply too busy to give it any more than a passing thought.

And I was content.

CHAPTER ELEVEN

*K*ris sank into a chair and stared at the High Elf, his blue eyes dark with pain. "So what happened?" he gasped out.

Niklas wiped at his leathery, lined cheeks and blew his nose. "We're not sure yet," he managed finally.

"But they're dead?"

"Dead." More tears welled up from the dark eyes as Niklas shook his grey head. "Dead."

Through my own tears, I saw Kris slide to his knees beside the aged Elf and wrap his arms around the slight, shaking shoulders. "Oh, my friend, I'm so sorry!" he said brokenly.

For several minutes, only our sobs could be heard in the still room.

"How could this happen?" Kris said at last. "How did we get to this?"

"One small step at a time," I said. "One unanswered insult and then another."

"One lost bit of freedom," Niklas said, straightening and scrubbing at his face. "And then one more."

Kris sat back on his heels and looked at the aged Elf. "Allowing one group to feel superior to another."

Again, Niklas nodded. "And act superior," he said.

Kris sighed and returned to his seat. He reached out and briefly gripped the Elf's two hands. "I am so sorry, Niklas," he said. "For your loss and for failing to . . ."

Niklas shook his head. "You didn't fail us, Kris," he said softly. "We failed ourselves."

I snorted. An unladylike sound, Mama would have told me, but expressive. "How could people as gentle as you be called to blame?" I said.

"By failing to act," Niklas said. "By allowing things to go on as we did. By . . . caring too much." He raised reddened eyes to us. "We could have done something. In the early days. When Kris first began his campaign."

"Oh, Niklas, that was nearly fifty years ago!" Kris said.

I shook my head. Had it really been fifty years ago?

"Yes, well, you were on the right track then, and if we'd allowed you to continue, we probably wouldn't be facing this disaster now," Niklas said.

Kris's mouth twisted. "My way was causing you more pain," he said.

"Yes, then. But a small amount of pain compared

to . . . now." Niklas put his hands over his face.

"Like pulling a rotten tooth," I said. "Painful at the time, but infinitely better than leaving it."

"Yes. We should have pulled that particular tooth many, many years ago."

"But what could you have done?" Kris said. "You were, quite literally, outweighed by the humans."

Niklas smiled slightly. "You are forgetting Elf magic," he said.

"Yes, well, I'm still struggling to understand it," Kris said.

"And that too is our fault."

"Let's stop talking about who is at fault," I said.

"You're exactly right, my dear," Kris said. "What we need to do now is collect facts and decide what's to be done."

"My thoughts precisely," I said.

There was a knock at the door.

Kris looked up. "Come!" he said.

It swung slowly inwards. Agathe stood there.

"They've come," she said. "From the . . ." She shook her head and disappeared.

Kris quickly got to his feet and left the room. Niklas was close behind him.

I followed them slowly, coming to a stop in the center of the wide hallway.

The front door stood open. A swirl of snow skittered across the floor nearly to my slippers.

"We've come . . ." an Elf voice began, then stopped abruptly.

"We've collected the . . . the . . . bodies," a second voice said.

"So there's no doubt," Niklas said.

"None, High Elf."

Niklas fell against the wall beside the door and dropped his head into his hands. "Ah, my children!" he said.

Kris gripped the small shoulder with one hand. "Do we know what happened?" he said, swinging the door wider and waving the two Elves inside. "Come in, my brothers, out of the cold."

The Elves shook snow from their shoulders and stepped into the warmth and light of the hallway.

As the light fell on them, I recognized first Knut and then his younger brother, Otto.

Kris closed the door and turned to them.

"Yes, we know quite a bit more," Knut said. "We know it was murder."

"Murder?" I gasped.

"As good as," Otto said. "The three Elves were ordered to go up on the roof and reattach the gutters."

"The heavy snowfall last week had torn one end out

of its mooring," Knut said. "And the owner was worried that the whole thing was going to come down."

"So he sent those young Elves up on that roof?" Kris said. "In those temperatures?"

"And completely without any safety measures," Knut said.

We stared at him. I could picture the scene. Three young Elves, without any form of harness to secure them to the roof, scampering about on a frozen, ice-slippery tin roof four stories above the solidly frozen earth.

I sank into a nearby chair. Knut was right. It *was* murder.

"Come into the study," Kris said. He turned to me. "Becs, could you bring something hot?" he said.

I nodded and got to my feet, almost running into Agathe, who was carrying a large tray with several steaming cups on it.

"Ah, Agathe. Ever watchful," Kris said. "Bring it in, dear, bring it in."

I followed and resumed the chair I had so recently vacated.

The others found places to sit.

After Agathe had served each of us a steaming hot cup of cider and set a large dish of freshly-baked cookies on the nearest table, she tucked the tray under her arm. "It there anything else I can bring, Master Kris?"

Kris shook his head and smiled at her. "Nothing, Agathe," he said. "And you're welcome to stay if you wish."

Agathe shook her head. "I'd better take this news in small batches," she said, her eyes welling with tears. "Just call if you need anything."

"We will, Agathe. Thank you."

She nodded and left the room.

Kris took a deep breath, then turned to Knut and Otto. "So?"

"Well, as nearly as we can figure, Simon lost his footing first and Sven tried to catch him. Then the two of them slid into Thomas. By then, a brick wall couldn't have stopped them. They slid right off the place where the gutter had been attached and fell four stories onto the rocks of the drive."

"Did they . . . suffer?" Kris asked.

I turned to look at him, then felt a pang.

Certainly he had changed, as I had. His blond hair was completely white and he had a snowy white beard to match. And his tall, active figure was somewhat shorter and considerably heavier now.

But the lines in his face were usually happy lines, carved there by his permanent smile.

But tonight, for the first time, I realized that my husband was looking every inch his sixty-seven years.

New lines had formed and his normally ruddy, healthy skin was a dead gray.

"Thomas died immediately. Sven a short time later."

"And Simon?"

"Simon was unconscious but still breathing until they got him to the stable. He stopped shortly afterwards."

"The stable?" I said.

"The master wouldn't allow them to be brought into the hotel."

Kris's face was no longer gray. Now it was suffused with color. "Wouldn't allow—" He stood up, both of his large, powerful hands clenched into fists. "Are you telling me that the man who ordered them up onto that roof didn't even have the decency to try to help them after the accident?"

Knut and Otto stared at him. This was a Kris they had never seen before.

"Well . . . yes, Master Kris," Knut said. "I'm afraid that's exactly what happened."

Kris took a deep breath and deliberately spread out his fingers. Then he moved back to his chair and sat once more.

"Please excuse me," he said, taking another deep, calming breath.

He turned to Niklas. "We have to do something."

Niklas nodded. He looked at the other two Elves. "I'm afraid that Kris and I will have a lot of discussing to do, brothers," he said. "You are welcome to listen in if you want, but I think there are more pressing matters that you need to take care of." He glanced at the door.

"Yes, High Elf," Knut said, getting up and pulling Otto to his feet. "We have some sad duties to take care of." He looked first at Niklas, then Kris.

"You must know that the People are ready for rebellion," Knut said, quietly. "None of us are going to just let this pass."

Kris nodded. "Then it'll be war," he said.

"We're ready, if that's what it comes to. We'll fight. Like our brothers across the ocean."

They bowed slightly and left.

"He's talking about the conflict between those United States, isn't he?" Niklas said, looking at Kris.

Kris nodded. "He is. They too are fighting for fundamental rights. Pray it doesn't come to that here." He looked at Niklas. "We have to do something, old friend," he said.

"Yes," Niklas said sadly. "Yes, you're right, Kris. Before the Elves forget themselves completely and resort to conflict, we must do something."

Several hours later, I carried in yet another tray of cider, this time with thick sandwiches and some fruit preserves.

"I think we've eliminated every single country on the planet," Kris said, leaning his elbows on the map spread out before him on the table. "Oh, thank you, dear." He reached for a sandwich and mug. "Resettling your people in a safe place is proving to be more complicated than either of us realized."

"I think you're right," Niklas said, reaching for the remaining plate.

They chewed silently for a few moments, their eyes still on the map.

"Well, maybe . . . no, that wouldn't work." Niklas sighed.

"The only place left is the North Pole," Kris said, stabbing with a long finger.

Niklas froze with his sandwich raised to his mouth. He stared at Kris.

Kris stopped chewing. "Niklas, I was joking," he said.

Still Niklas stared.

"Niklas? I didn't mean it!"

For several moments, the old Elf remained motionless. Finally, he lowered his sandwich to the plate, deliberately wiped his hands and lips on his serviette, and cleared his throat. "Kris, I think you've hit on the solution!" he said.

"Niklas, I said I was only joking!"

The old Elf nodded. "I know you did," he said.

"What are you thinking, Niklas?" Kris said. "The North Pole is just ice and snow. Nothing grows. Nothing could survive."

"*We* could survive," Niklas said softly. He looked at Kris. "And isn't that the point?"

"How? How could the Elves survive?" Kris said.

"Once again, you are forgetting Elf magic," Niklas said.

"Elf magic can keep people alive in that inhospitable climate?"

"Most certainly." The old Elf smiled.

"Well, now I've heard everything!"

"You keep saying that," Niklas said, his smile widening, "but I don't think it's true!"

"But . . ."

"Trust me on this, Kris, old friend. We could not only survive, but thrive!"

"Well, I know that Elves are hardy, but . . ."

"I'm not just talking about the Elves, Kris," Niklas said quietly.

"You—you're . . . who are you talking about?" Kris looked at the old Elf suspiciously.

Niklas's smile grew wider. "Only the best friends that we Elves have ever had. You and Mary Rebecca."

Now both Kris and I were staring at him.

"You think Kris and I could survive in that cold climate?" I said.

Niklas turned to look at me. "Do you trust me, Becca?" he said.

I blinked.

"Do you?"

I smiled. "You know I do, Niklas. With my life."

He smiled. "As I do you." He looked at Kris and put a small, gnarled hand on his sleeve. "We couldn't do it without you, my brother," he said.

"But how could we go?" Kris said. "So many people depend on us."

"There is nothing that your humanitarian company couldn't continue to handle, Kris," Niklas said. "Your human overseers have been taking more and more of the responsibility since Becca's parents were killed in that accident ten years ago, and you had to take over her father's company."

"That's another thing. Becca's father's company."

"Sell it," I said.

Kris turned to look at me. "What did you say?"

"I said sell it, Kris. It has no sentimental value for me. It had none for Papa. It was just the company that

he ran. A means to an end. It was *your* company that he loved."

"Are you saying that you'd like to go?" Kris was staring at me.

"Yes, I think I am," I said, shrugging my shoulders. "Our foster children have grown and started their own lives. And even though we have many special friends here, none are more precious than the Elves. I can't bear the thought of them leaving without me."

He was silent for a moment. "But what about our annual Christmas Eve toy run? It has grown so. I'm sure that many, many children would notice if it just . . . stopped."

Niklas smiled again. "Why would it have to stop?" he said.

"You mean you . . . you . . . what do you mean?" Kris frowned.

"We can build the toys and gifts anywhere, with the right facilities," Niklas said.

"And you could find the right facilities *at the North Pole?*"

"Most certainly. Because we will take the most important thing with us. *Us.*"

"Us."

"Our heart. Our love. Our skill. All of our gifts from the Father Creator."

"But what about delivery? Won't that pose a bit of a problem?"

"That will be the easiest part of all." Niklas grinned.

"That part would be easy?" Kris said softly. "That I would have to see."

"It can be done, Kris," I said, putting a hand on his arm. "I know it."

Kris looked from Niklas to me and back again. He shook his head. "I can't believe what I'm hearing," he said.

Niklas chuckled. "Well, believe it, my friend," he said. "Because it's going to happen."

"I haven't said yes yet."

"Oh, but you will!"

CHAPTER TWELVE

*K*ris, I'm sixty-four years old. I can't believe that I'm going to start over. At my age!"

We were sitting in the sleigh, loaded with everything I thought we would need in our new home at the North Pole—mostly warm stuff.

Kris laughed. "Trust you to get right to the heart of the matter, Becs," he said. He looked up.

A gray, uniformly cloudy sky stretched from horizon to horizon.

"Great day for traveling," he said, grinning. "Another bit of good fortune to make the leaving easier."

"Yes. It's all been surprisingly easy," I said. "Selling everything. Transferring responsibilities." I glanced over to the right. "But I do seem to be having trouble parting from the people. And the places."

I looked at the large group, made up mostly of our foster children and their families, who stood waving good-bye from the front walk.

"Oh, I don't know if I can do this," I said, reaching for my handkerchief.

Kris smiled at me. "Oh, you can, my dear!" he said. "Show me some of that famous Kringle courage!"

"The Kringle courage has mostly evaporated."

"I don't have to remind you that you—"

"Wanted this. No, you don't," I said, dabbing at my eyes, "and I know it is the right thing to do for so many reasons. It's just . . . my family."

"We can come back to visit," I said.

"Niklas tells me that is true, and my head agrees with him. I just don't know how all of this is going to work, and my head is having a hard time explaining things to my heart."

Kris laughed. "You'll just have to keep on trying, dear," he said.

He clicked at the team. "Let's go, boys!"

The horses leaned into the harness and the heavy sleigh started forward smoothly, following the tracks worn into the fresh snow by the countless sleighs of the Elves that had preceded us earlier that morning.

There was a loud cheer from behind us and I turned to see everyone waving white hankies.

I waved until the sleigh turned the corner, hiding the group from me. Then I settled into the seat beside Kris and sighed.

"Well, we're off," I said, rather tearfully.

"Here's to new adventures, Becs," he said, grinning.

I snuggled up against him. "I wonder what all the humans thought when they woke up this morning and had to cook their own breakfasts."

He chuckled, that warm, rich chuckle I loved. "Not to mention the feeding of the animals and all of the other chores that are such a part of daily living. I guess we'll never know. But it would have been entertaining to see."

He went on, "Maybe the poorer families will be able to find work now."

I stared up at him. "But of course. Why didn't I think of that before?"

"What? That the poorer people could take the places of the Elves?"

"Yes. It's so logical. And their masters won't be able to treat them as slaves."

"No, we have that to cling to. The laws regarding the treatment of humans are too well entrenched."

I smiled and snuggled closer to his warm frame.

"So, do you have any idea where we are going?"

"Well, I'm not entirely certain," Kris said, shrugging. "Niklas told me, quite specifically, that we needed to follow the Main Trunk Road across the bridge, then into the field there."

I shook my head. "Okay. Then what?"

"I really don't know. Maybe that is a mustering point."

"Pretty poor planning for our great new start."

He laughed. "I trust Niklas," he said simply.

I sighed. "I do too."

It was still early and cold. We quickly moved through the city. We had almost reached the outskirts when we came upon a knot of people, standing in the street.

Kris halted the team a short distance away and got out.

Someone toward the middle of the group was talking loudly. "Well, something has to be done about it!" he was saying.

"Yes!" someone else shouted. "They have to be taught a lesson!"

There was a general murmur of assent.

"What is the matter?" Kris asked a man who was standing on the edge of the group.

"The Elves have disappeared," the man said.

"Which Elves?"

"All of them."

"All of the Elves?"

"It looks that way."

"Well, imagine that!" Kris looked at me and winked.

"Apparently, someone saw a sleigh full of them driving along the street in this direction," the man said.

"Really?"

"Well, you know that Elves aren't allowed the use of the animals. And definitely not allowed to drive," the man said. "At least not without a human in the vehicle."

"Oh, yes. I did realize that," Kris said.

"So, of course a group of concerned citizens tried to follow them," the man said. "Things like this cannot be allowed!"

"Oh, definitely not," Kris said mildly.

"Sir, I don't believe you appreciate the gravity of this situation!"

"I don't believe I do," Kris said, grinning. "Some people are going to have to learn how to do things for themselves. Tragedy!"

He walked back to the sleigh and got in.

The man was watching him. He glanced at our piled sled.

"Wait!" he shouted. He started to walk toward us.

Other people in the crowd turned and looked in our direction.

A second man stared at Kris intently. "Hey!" he said. He too started toward us. "Hey, I know you!"

Even from where I sat, I could see the old scar on the man's cheek.

"Uh-oh," Kris said, grinning at me. "I guess we know what happened to Klein." He clucked to the team. "We'd better hurry, fellas," he said.

The horses leaped into action, starting the sleigh with a jerk that nearly sent my warm hat into the piled-up backseat.

"Wait a moment!" Both men were still moving toward us and had sped up.

"Good-bye!" Kris said, waving cheerfully as the horses veered slightly to avoid a collision.

"Stop!"

Their shouting had attracted the attention of more of the group.

Everyone turned to stare.

"He knows something!" Klein said, pointing at us.

More of the people were starting to move in our direction.

"I think we'd better take a different route," Kris said.

Almost without his direction, the team turned down a side road and leaned into their harness as they increased the pace.

"Stop them!" someone was shouting.

"I think it's a race!" Kris said, looking down at me and grinning.

I stared at him. "Aren't you worried?"

"Not a bit," he said, laughing. "Trust in the Father Creator."

"But, Kris, He isn't here!"

"That doesn't mean He isn't helping!" he said.

He stood up. "Come on, boys! Let's show them what you've got!" he said to the team.

The horses took a corner so fast that the heavy sleigh followed on one runner.

"Whoop! Hang on, Becs!" Kris said.

I could hear harness bells behind us.

Kris glanced back. "Uh-oh, they've called out the militia!"

I turned and tried to see over the mound of household goods in the back. Two small, single-horse cutters were coming around the corner and were obviously gaining.

"Hang on, Becs. Here's another corner!"

The words were barely out of his mouth before I could feel the sleigh begin to tip to the other side.

"Kris, I'm too old for this!" I said.

He laughed his great, rolling burst of sound. "Ho, ho, ho! Never, never too old, Becs!" he said.

The sleigh settled onto two runners again. I glanced around. We were once more on the main route. I could see the bridge ahead of us.

I glanced up at my husband of nearly fifty years.

He was standing in the sleigh, feathering the reins. Long, white hair was streaming back in the wind of our passage and his face, where his thick white beard and moustache allowed, was glowing red in the crisp air.

Laughing, he hollered encouraging words to the team.

He was . . . enjoying this.

"Kris, you're crazy!" I said. Then gasped and grabbed for my hat as it once again made a bid for freedom.

"This is living, Becs!" he said. "Living!"

I heard the change in the sound of the horses' hoofs as they hit the wooden boards of the bridge.

For just a moment, I remembered that fateful day so long ago when Kris had brought me here and changed my life.

Then the horses were once more running on the hard-packed snow of the road. They were puffing now. Great clouds of vapor streamed out behind them.

"Just a little farther, boys!" Kris said. "There it is!"

The horses seemed to understand him because they put on a burst of speed.

I glanced around again, half-rising to my feet to see.

The two small sleighs had been joined by several men on horseback. None of them seemed to be trying to overtake us, but they weren't letting the distance between us grow, either.

I sat down once more. "They're just following," I said.

"They're planning on our team tiring out," Kris said. "But we're not tired, are we, boys?"

The team put on yet another burst of speed, and Kris laughed again.

"See?" he said.

The team turned suddenly into a field, following several sets of sled tracks in the deep snow.

I stared. Milling about the field were many, many teams of horses. Still harnessed. They stood and watched us, then scattered when we got closer.

"What's going on here?" I said.

"Here we are, Becs," Kris said. "Hold on! I'm not sure what's going to happen!"

His last words echoed weirdly and, for a moment, it was as though we had driven into a tunnel. The wind stopped and, just for a moment, I felt almost . . . breathless . . . as though we had gone down a sudden rise.

I grabbed onto Kris and closed my eyes.

Then the team stopped.

I opened my eyes and blinked at the sudden bright sunshine. Then I glanced around. Everything about us was still and white, sparkling in the light. A perfect blue bowl of sky curved over us.

I frowned. Wait a minute. It had been cloudy.

And where were the trees? Where was the bridge? They should have been . . . right . . .

I looked up at Kris and found his eyes on me.

"Figured it out yet?" he asked.

"We're here?"

"Just like that," he said, grinning. He looked around. "Not sure what to do from here, but I'm fairly certain that Niklas will have everything figured out."

Just then, we heard the sound of bells.

I saw a sleigh with a team of eight pulling it coming toward us.

I frowned. Something about the sleigh was . . .

"Um, Kris?"

He laughed. "Okay, here's something you don't see every day," he said. "A flying sleigh."

I looked again. Yes. That was it. The sleigh wasn't riding along on the white snow. It was hovering just above it.

I scrambled out of the seat and gripped my husband's arm. "Kris, what is it?"

"If I'm not mistaken, it's Niklas, taking care of us."

The sleigh touched down and then, for the first time, I turned to look at the team pulling it.

These weren't horses! They were . . . deer.

"Kris, those are deer."

"I noticed that, Becs," he said, laughing. "Reindeer, I think. Marvelous!"

"And they're flying."

"I noticed that too."

The creatures landed softly and moved gracefully toward us.

I hid behind my husband.

Okay, I'm not a coward but . . . okay, I'm a coward.

"Hugh! How nice of you to come for us!" Kris said.

I peeked around him. Here was something familiar.

Hugh leaped lightly from the other sleigh and walked over to us. "Niklas figured you'd get here about now," he said, holding out one hand.

"Well, he was right, again," Kris said, shaking it.

"Any problems?"

"Oh, nothing important," Kris said.

I looked at him. Nothing important!

"Close your mouth, Becs. You look silly," Kris said.

I snapped my mouth shut.

"Mrs. Kris, how was the trip?" Hugh said.

"Fast," I said, elbowing Kris in the ribs.

"We made record time," Kris said, laughing.

Right. Record time. I elbowed him again.

"Well, at least you arrived safely," Hugh said. "Let's get you unhitched and squared away."

The two of them quickly unhooked our team.

Then Kris led the horses back the way we had come. I followed, then frowned as I realized that the snow was completely unmarked only a few feet behind the sleigh. I glanced up at the sky. It was as though we descended— sleigh, team and all—from up there.

Kris said something to the off-lead horse.

The animal snorted and started forward.

And suddenly, they were gone. All of them. In a blink.

I know. Because I blinked.

"What?" I looked at Kris. "Where did they go?"

Kris smiled at me. "Back," he said.

"Back?" I was having a hard time keeping up.

"Back home. We really couldn't keep a team of horses at the North Pole, could we?"

I shook my head. "I suppose not," I said, uncertainly.

But I suddenly understood why all of the unattended teams of horses had been standing there in the field just outside of town.

Kris laughed. "Let's get this other team hitched."

Hugh had already backed his sleigh up in front of ours, pulled our tree under his sleigh, and secured it. Now he was busily attaching chains to the front of our sleigh.

"Well, you've almost finished," Kris said, slapping the Elf on the shoulder. "I can see that if I drag my feet just a bit more, I'll never have to work again!"

Hugh laughed. "I know that will never happen, Master Kris," he said.

"Hugh, this is a new life for us. And I want to set the new rules now. There is no one here who can make your life miserable if they hear you addressing me by my given name, right?"

"Right," Hugh grinned.

"Then I want no more titles between us, all right? From here on, you are Hugh and I am Kris. Just Kris. Got that?"

"I do Mas . . . Kris," Hugh said, his grin widening.

"Good," Kris said, smiling. "Now let me meet our team."

Hugh finished fastening the chains and moved with Kris toward the lead animal.

"This is Dasher," Hugh said, placing a hand on the animal's withers. "He's the grandpapa of the team."

The lead deer snorted and stamped a hoof. Then he swung his heavy antlers and knocked Hugh into the snow.

"Oof!" Hugh said, laughing. "These senior citizens are touchy!"

Another snort.

Kris stepped forward and bowed slightly. "Pleased to make your acquaintance, Dasher!" he said.

The deer nodded and closed one eye. Then he glanced at Hugh, who was just getting to his feet, and shook his head.

"I know. I have to work with him too," Kris whispered loudly.

"Hey!" Hugh said.

Kris laughed and the deer wheezed softly.

Was the animal laughing too? I stared.

"I'd like you to meet my lovely bride," Kris said to the deer.

It turned and looked at me and bowed its head.

I nodded too, feeling at once privileged and frightened.

I guess I simply wasn't accustomed to introductions involving animals. And certainly not animals who came equipped with weapons on their heads.

Suddenly, Dasher raised its head and sniffed the wind. Then it looked at Hugh and snorted softly.

"Better wait until after we get there to meet the others," Hugh said. "Dasher says there's a storm coming fast!"

Kris and I were directed into the front sleigh with Hugh, who picked up the reins. "Don't dawdle, Dasher!" he said.

The team sprang forward and, in a flash, we were bouncing along on the top of the snow. Then the two runners left the ground entirely, and, for the first time in my life, I was flying.

It was both exhilarating and frightening. I held onto Kris's arm.

"If we crash, I'm not going to be much protection," he chuckled into my ear.

My grip tightened, and he laughed.

"Have it your way!" he said.

Soon we were looking down at the snow-covered ground.

I glanced around. Far away, below and behind us, I could make out an enormous white cloud, which seemed to be following us.

"Is that the storm?" I said to Kris, pointing.

He glanced around. "Must be," he said.

He turned back to Hugh. "I think it's gaining," he said.

Hugh too looked behind us. "Better put on some speed, Dasher, old boy!" he said.

I suddenly felt as though we had left important things in the air behind us.

Along with my warm hat.

I clapped my hand to my head. "Oh, my hat!" I said.

Kris laughed. "How much farther?" he shouted to Hugh. "Becs just lost her hat!"

Hugh pointed down below us. "It's just there!" he said.

We followed the pointing finger.

Directly below us was a little settlement, complete with long, log buildings and smoke-belching chimneys.

"Okay, admit it. You didn't just build that this morning, did you?" Kris said.

Hugh laughed. "As soon as we knew where we were going, all available Elves and Elfas were dispatched here!" he shouted into the wind. "Hold on, now! We're descending."

The deer had started down in a steep spiral. I clung tighter to Kris's arm.

"I hope we land soon," he said, "while I still have use of my hand!"

I ignored him.

Soon, the reindeer had flattened out their dive and were skimming along just above the ground, closer and closer. Until, finally, I felt the sleigh runners touch the snow.

Then the deer slowed to a smooth stop. Kris jumped out and quickly lifted me down.

"Let's get everyone under cover!" he said.

He ran to Dasher. "What can I do to help, Dasher?" he said.

The deer turned and looked at him, then shook its head and looked at me.

"Becca will come too," Kris said. "Where do we go?"

The deer started off, with Hugh, Kris, and I running alongside.

"Good thing I'm not an old woman or this would be really tough," I said, puffing.

"What?" Hugh said.

"Just keep running!" Kris said, laughing.

Dasher led us to one of the larger buildings. A wide door slid open just as we reached it. Two more Elves waved us inside.

Kris stood aside for Dasher to lead his team in, then grabbed my mittened hand and led me into the dim interior.

EPILOGUE

"So that was how everything started," Dorothy said. "How you and we Elves ended up here."

"Yes," Rebecca said, getting up and poking the fire. She glanced at the carved wooden clock on the mantle. "Oh, my, look at the time! Kris will be back soon and I haven't even started his breakfast!"

Dorothy too glanced at the clock. "Are we finished?" she asked.

"Only if you want to be," Rebecca said, smiling. "But there's more to tell. "Why don't you follow me into the kitchen and we'll keep going?"

Dorothy gathered her papers and stood up. "Lead on," she said, smiling.

Rebecca led her back into the front hall, then through another doorway into a large, warm kitchen.

She snapped on the electric lights.

The room was dominated by a huge iron stove at the far end and by an enormous table in the center.

Rebecca bustled over to the stove and, opening the door, poked at the fire. "Just set your things there," she said. "On the table."

Dorothy settled herself at the table. "I'm ready," she said, "but I have one question, first."

"What is that, dear?" Rebecca said.

"Well, you've had electricity for years," Dorothy said. "Why don't you install one of the big electric stoves?"

Rebecca straightened and put her hands on her hips. "What? Don't you know that everything tastes better when it's cooked in a wood stove?"

"I guess I do now," Dorothy said, smiling.

"Huh. Electric stove," Rebecca mumbled. She began to pull things from her neat cupboards.

She set them on the table. "Now where were we in our story?" she said.

"You had just arrived," Dorothy said.

"Oh, yes. Just ahead of the storm." Rebecca rolled up her long sleeves and started adding ingredients to a large bowl.

"Well, we were welcomed by all of the Elves and introduced to the existing members of the North Pole community."

"The reindeer and the polar bears?"

"Yes. Them. And the seals and walruses."

"They have all been integral in the work that goes on here," Dorothy said.

"Oh, yes, my dear! We couldn't have accomplished nearly what we have without their help!"

"But the Elves were the major contributors?"

Rebecca smiled. "You know that, without our brothers, we couldn't have done anything. Certainly we couldn't possibly have built up the Christmas Eve toy and gift run to what it is now."

"It covers the globe!" Dorothy said.

"Exactly!" Rebecca smiled. "It is the most important thing in Kris's life," she said softly.

"Apart from you," Dorothy said.

Rebecca laughed. "I suppose that's true."

Dorothy frowned. "I have to ask you something, Rebecca," she said.

"Go right ahead," Rebecca said, smiling.

"Well, it's rather delicate . . ."

"You're wondering about my age, aren't you?" Rebecca said.

"Umm . . . yes."

"To tell you the truth, I'm not sure I quite understand it either," Rebecca said. "I know that Kris and I were married in 1810."

"And came here in 1857," Dorothy said.

"Right."

"At about the age of sixty-four . . ."

"I know what you're getting at. This is 2012. That would make us . . . rather old."

"To put it mildly."

Rebecca laughed. "Well, Dorothy, I don't question it too closely. Niklas promised us that he would help us accomplish the things we most wanted to. And he has. I assume that it is Elf Magic that has kept us from aging since we came here."

"I do know a bit about Elf Magic," Dorothy said.

"I should hope so," Rebecca said, laughing. She looked around the warm, welcoming room. "It is what makes everything work, here," she said quietly. "It is how the Elves accomplish so much in the work sheds. How goods are shipped here. How the reindeer fly. How Kris is able to reach so many homes in a single night." She snorted softly. "Heavens! It is how we grow our food! How we survive!"

Dorothy wrote busily for a moment. Finally, she lifted her head. "But what is it?" she said. "What is Elf Magic?"

Rebecca smiled. "That, I do know, my dear," she said softly. "It is the power of perfect love. Something the Elves were given by the Father Creator, and something we are still trying to learn from the Elves."

Sudden sounds from outside intruded into the quiet room.

"Oh-oh! Sounds like Kris is back!" Rebecca said, smiling. "Let's go welcome him home!"

DISSCUSSION QUESTIONS

1. *What do we learn about Kris during his and Rebecca's very first encounter?*

2. *What qualities would you ascribe to Kris? Rebecca? The Elves?*

3. *How would you describe the Elf community? The human community?*

4. *How does Kris change in the ensuing years? Rebecca? The Elves?*

5. *Can the power of love change the world?*